Tales from China's Classic Essential Readings

中国蒙学经典故事丛书

# Tales from the Children's Knowledge Treasury

# 《幼学琼林》故事

张 梅 *Zhang Mei*◎著

畅国杰 *Chang Guojie*◎译

CHINA INTERCONTINENTAL PRESS

五洲传播出版社

# 前言

中国古代重视对儿童和青少年的教育，产生了多种流传很广的启蒙读物，以使学生加强修养，增长智慧。《三字经》《百家姓》《千字文》和《幼学琼林》就是这些蒙学读物中的佼佼者，它们的主要功能是使学生认识汉字，并对他们进行文化和品德教育。

这些蒙学读物内容通俗易懂，形式简单，读起来很像歌谣，非常适合读者朗读和背诵。对很多中国人来说，这些读物是对他们一生影响最大的书籍，他们通过这些读物认识汉字，了解中国的历史、地理、社会等多方面的知识，并受到品德教育。直到今天，中国人仍然喜爱和重视这些蒙学读物。

上面提到的四本书中，《千字文》产生最早，是南北朝时梁朝人编写的，4个字一句，共250句，1000个字，所以称为“千字文”。

《三字经》产生于宋代，并经过后人的修改。它每句3个字，所以叫“三字经”。全书总共约500句，其中讲的许多观念和道理，对中国人影响深远。《三字经》已经被联合国教科文组织选入儿童道德修养的必读书目，译成多国文字，在全世界范围内发行。

《百家姓》也产生于宋代，是有关中国人姓氏的启蒙读物，采用4个字一句的歌谣形式，共计568字，介绍了504个中国人的姓氏。

《幼学琼林》在这四本书里产生最晚，是明朝人编写的。它内容极为丰富，几乎是一部小型的自然和社会百科全书，所以有人说“读了《幼学》走天下”。

这些书中蕴藏着丰厚的中华民族历史文化传统，尤其是其中提到的那些隽永、生动的故事，令读者印象深刻。“中国蒙学经典故事”丛书从上述四本书中精选出一些在中国广泛流传的故事，以简短而生动有趣的文字讲述出来，通过它们，向全世界广大的读者介绍中华民族的历史文化知识和思想、道德观念。书中的故事分成若干现代人容易理解的类型，并配以幽默生动的漫画。

这套丛书不仅适合儿童和青少年，也适合广大对中国文化感兴趣、初步接触中国历史文化的读者。

# Preface

The ancient China long ago has stressed on the child and youth education. Many primer readings spreading far and beyond came into focus, thus strengthening the cause of child upbringing and brightness. *The Three Character Classic, the Hundreds Surnames, the Thousand Character Classic, and the Children's Knowledge Treasury* are the best examples of such primer readings. Their main goal is to enable the child to learn characters and educate them about culture and morality.

The readings are easy to understand, and simple to read and recite as they resemble songs. They influenced the lives of many Chinese. They learned Chinese, as well as gaining knowledge on Chinese history, geography, and society. They are well-educated on morality too. Till today, Chinese still love and stress these readings.

Of the above-mentioned four books, *the Thousand Character Classic* came out earliest. It was compiled by a man of the Liang Dynasty. With four characters in each sentence, there are 250 sentences and 1,000 characters in the book. Due to this reason, the book is titled *the Thousand Character Classic*.

*The Three Character Classic* came out during the Song Dynasty times and was modified later. As it has three characters in each sentence, the book is titled the Three Character Classic. It comprises about 500 sentences. Many ideas and truths in it have profound impact on the Chinese people. UNESCO incorporated the book into a list of compulsory books dedicated for the child moral education. It was translated into many languages and circulated globally.

*The Hundreds Surnames* came out during the Song Dynasty times. It is a primer reading related to the Chinese surnames. With a total of 568 characters and in the form of songs with four characters in each sentence, it introduced 504 Chinese surnames in all.

*The Children's Knowledge Treasury* came out the latest. The people of Ming Dynasty compiled this book. With rich contents, it became a mini-encyclopeadia of natural and social sciences. It owns the reputation of "Making you knowledgeable enough after reading *the Children's Knowledge Treasury*".

We can see profound historical and cultural traditions clearly in these books - especially those vivid and meaningful tales greatly impress the readers. *Tales from China's Classic Essential Readings* has selected tales spreading far and beyond in China from the above four books and tells them in short, lively and interesting truths. Readers, around the world, can learn the historical and cultural knowledge of the Chinese nation, ideology and morality through them. The tales are divided into categories to be easily understood by modern people, with the support of humorous and vivid cartoons.

The books are not only suitable for children and youth, but also for readers with interest in Chinese culture. They can experience the contact with Chinese history and culture.

# Contents
## 目录

## 历史故事
## Historical Tales

## 美德故事
Tales of Virtue



## 人才故事
Tales of Talents

# Tales of Chinese Idioms

# 成语故事

# 杞人忧天

原文：

xīn duō guò lǜ， hé yì qǐ rén yōu tiān
心多过虑，何异杞人忧天

故事：

杞（qǐ）国是中国古代的一个小诸侯国，经常受到强大的邻国的压迫和侵略。杞国人经常生活在忧患之中，担心自己的国家随时会遭到什么不幸。

这个国家有一个人，每天都害怕天会掉下来，地会塌下去，他想，如果真的发生了这样的灾难，就没有什么地方可以躲避了。因为总想着这些可怕的事情，他愁得睡不着觉，吃不下饭，身体和精神都很虚弱。

有一位朋友见他这样忧虑不安，为他的健康而担心，就跑来开导他说："天不过是聚集在一起的气体罢了，天地之间到处都是这种气体，你每天伸展身体、俯仰、呼吸，其实都是生活在这种气体当中。既然如此，你为什么还要担心天会塌下来呢？”

杞人听了朋友这番话，仍然不放心，追问道：“如果天真的是由某种气体聚集在一起形成的，那么太阳、月亮和无数的星辰都挂在上面，它们难道就不会掉下来吗？”

朋友回答：“太阳、月亮和星辰也是由气体聚集而成

的，只是它们会发光罢了。即使它们掉下来，也不会砸伤我们的。”

关于天的问题总算解决了，但杞人马上又问：“如果大地塌陷下去，我们怎么办？”朋友耐心地解释说：“大地不过是堆积在一起的泥土和石块罢了。这些泥土、石块到处都是，塞满了大地上的每一个角落。你每天都在大地上面站立、走路、奔跑、跺脚，也没有发生什么事，为什么还要担心它会塌陷下去呢？”

经过朋友这么一番开导，这个杞人才放下心来，开始快快乐乐地生活，该吃饭就吃饭，该睡觉就睡觉。而那个开导他的朋友也放心了，高高兴兴地走了。后来人们就用“杞人忧天”这个成语来比喻不必要的或者是缺乏根据的忧虑和担心。

杞人害怕天会掉下来、地会塌下去这件事传到了一位哲人耳朵里，引发了他的思考。他想，如果天确实是聚集在一起的气体，大地确实是堆积在一起的泥土和石块，那这些物质怎么可能不毁坏呢？当然，天地的毁坏应该是很久之后的事情了，但说它们不会毁坏是不对的。当天地毁坏时，那时候的人又怎么能不忧虑呢？这样说来，杞人的担忧也并非毫无道理。

# A Man of Qi Who Feared that the Sky Might Fall

Qi was a small kingdom in ancient China. It was often suppressed and invaded by strong neighbors and so the people of Qi often lived in suffering and misery, and worried that their country might encounter adversity at any time.

A man in the Kingdom of Qi feared the sky would fall and collapse onto the earth every day. He thought that if such a disaster really happened, there would be no place to run. Because he thought these dreadful things all the time, he couldn't sleep or eat food and his physical and mental condition became worse and worse.

Seeing that he was so restless and fearing for his health, a friend of his came over to explain to him, "In fact, the sky is actually a cluster of air and such air exists everywhere between the sky and the earth. You stretch your body, pitch and breathe every day in this kind of air. So, why do you worry about the sky falling?"

Even after hearing his friend's explanations, the man still couldn't get over his crippling fear. He then asked, "If the sky is really a cluster of air, won't the sun, the moon, and the stars fall down as they are just hunging there?"

The friend replied, "The sun, the moon and the stars are also clusters of air, the only difference is that they can give out brightness. Even if they do fall down, they will not hit us."

The man raised another question, "What shall we do if the earth collapses?" His friend explained patiently, "The earth is actually a pile of soil and stones. Such soil and stones can be seen everywhere on the earth. You stand, walk, run and stamp your foot on the earth every day, but nothing happens. So, how can it collapse?"

After hearing the painstaking simple explanations of his friend, the man finally relaxed and began to have a happy life with a good appetite and restful sleep. His friend was also relieved and happily left. Later, people used the four-character proverb to describe unnecessary or groundless worry or fear.

When a sage heard the story, the sage fell into deep consideration. He thought that if the sky really is a cluster of air and the earth is a pile of soil and stones, how can these substances be freed from destruction? Of course, the destruction of sky and earth will be a matter of many, many years from now and it's not right to say that they will be sound forever. When the sky and earth are really destroyed, will people have to worry about that? In such a sense, this man's worry is somewhat reasonable.

# 沧海桑田

原文：

cāng hǎi sāng tián wèi shì shì zhī duō biàn
沧 海 桑 田 ，谓 世 事 之 多 变

故事：

中国东汉（25—220）时候有个人叫蔡经，是个普通的平民，但仙人王方平认为他可以修行成为神仙，就教他变成神仙的方法。有一天，王方平告诉蔡经说，农历七月七日那天要到他家做客。蔡经赶紧让家人准备了很多酒菜，用来招待王方平的随从。

七月七日这天，王方平果然来到了蔡家。他坐在五条龙拉的车上，随从人员有好几百人，非常威风。演奏音乐的随从都乘坐着奇异的动物，从天上下来。到了蔡经家之后，那些随从人员就突然看不见了，蔡经一家人只看得见王方平。王方平派人去邀请仙女麻姑也到蔡经家来做客。过了一会儿，派出去的人回来报告说，麻姑说已经有五百多年没有见过王方

平了，但现在她正在巡视东海上的仙岛，等一会儿就亲自来见面。蔡经等人只能听到声音，看不到报信的人。

等了一会儿，听到有车马的声音，然后麻姑就从天上下来了。她的随从人员有王方平的一半那么多。蔡家人眼里的这位仙女，是个十八九岁的漂亮姑娘，长长的头发披散到腰间。她的衣服亮闪闪的，不知道是什么材料制成的。麻姑与王方平互相行礼后，就坐下来摆宴席。他们在酒席上使用的餐具都是用黄金和玉石制成的，里面盛放的菜肴大多是蔡经一家没有见过的奇花异果，香气传得很远。两位神仙又将一种肉干分给大家吃，说是用奇异的动物的肉做成的。

麻姑对王方平说："自从我修行成为神仙以来，已经看到东海的海水三次消失，变成农田。刚才到东海上的仙岛去巡视时，发现海水比以前浅了，只有上次所见到的一半。难道说东海又要变成陆地了吗？”王方平感慨地说：“圣人们都说，不久之后，东海又要变得干涸（hé），那里将变得尘土飞扬。”蔡经一家听到这番对话都十分惊讶，原来麻姑是个很长寿的仙女。以后人们提到“沧海桑田“这个成语，都用来比喻世事变化很大。

酒宴结束之后，麻姑去见蔡经家里的女性，赐祝福和礼物给她们。这中间发生了一个有意思的插曲。麻姑伸出手时，蔡经发现她的手不像人类的手，更像是鸟的爪子。他心想，背上很痒的时候，如果有这样一双鸟爪子似的手为自己抓痒，那该多舒服啊！王方平知道他心中在想什么，就让人把他拉到一边去鞭打，教训蔡经说：“麻姑是个仙女，你怎么敢有这种不好的想法呢？”蔡家人只看见有鞭子落在蔡经背上，而看不到拿鞭子执行王方平命令的人。王方平告诉蔡经说，这种鞭打也是在帮他修行，并不是什么人都可以得到的。

宴饮完毕，王方平和麻姑坐着各自的车辆、带着各自的随从，升天而去。仙人们走后，蔡家人发现他们所准备的几百瓶酒，已经被两位神仙那些看不见的随从人员喝光了。

# Seas Change into Mulberry Fields

During China's Eastern Han Dynasty (25–220) there was a common man named Cai Jing who the immortal Wang Fangping thought that could be taught and cultivated into an immortal. One day, Wang Fangping told Cai Jing that he would room with Cai's family on July 7th on the lunar calendar. Cai then immediately asked his family members to prepare many dishes and drinks to receive Wang Fangping's entourage.

To their surprise, Wang Fangping did in fact come to the Cai's home on July 7th. Seated in a chariot drawn by five dragons and with an enormous entourage, Wang looked very valiant. The musicians of the entourage were riding odd animals as they descended from the sky. As they reached Cai's home, the rest of the entourage disappeared suddenly and Cai's family members only saw Wang Fangping. Wang Fangping sent some of his people to invite the fairy lady Magu to guest in the Cai's as well. Shortly, the messenger came back and reported that Magu had said that she didn't see Wang Fangping for more than 500 years, but she was on an investigation tour of the fairy island on the East China Sea now and would come later. Cai Jing and his family members could only hear the voice of messenger but couldn't see him.

After a while, the sound of hooves and chariots were heard. Then Magu descended from the sky. Her entourage was half of that of Wang Fangping. Cai's family members saw that this fairy lady is a beautiful girl of about eighteen years old with long hair that fell to her waist. Her clothes were glistening, but they didn't know what fabric it was made of. After greeting each other, Magu and Wang Fangping sat down to have a meal. All of the tableware was made of gold and jade and most of the food placed in the tableware was mysterious blossoms and fruits with far-reaching fragrance never seen before by the Cai family. The two immortals also shared some jerky with the Cai family and told them that the jerky is made of the meat of bizarre animals.

Magu told Wang Fangping, "Since I turned into an immortal, I have seen the disappearance of sea water and the appearance of farm land in the East China Sea three times. I just found on my investigation tour on the fairy island in the East China Sea that the seawater is shallower than before and is only half of the level I saw last time. Will the East China Sea turn into a land once again?"

Wang Fangping sighed, "All immortals said that the East China Sea will dry up and clouds of dust flying up will be seen soon." The Cai's were surprised to know that Magu was an immortal fairy lady. Later

on, people used the proverb "Cang Hai Sang Tian" to describe the great changes.

After the meal, Magu came to see the female members of Cai's family and present blessings and gifts to them. When Magu stretched out her hand, Cai Jing found that her hand didn't resemble the hand of a human being, but instead resembled the claw of a bird. He thought that it would be very comfortable to scratch his own back with such a hand! Wang Fangping knew what Cai was thinking and asked his people to take Cai aside and whip him for his insolence, telling Cai Jing: "How can you have such evil intentions towards a fairy lady?" Cai's family members could only see the fall of the whip on Cai's back, but couldn't see the being responsible. Wang Fangping told Cai Jing, such kind of whipping is conducive to his cultivation and not all people can have such kind of privilege.

After the meal, Wang Fangping and Magu disappeared in the sky with their entourage by using their own talents. After the immortals left, Cai's family saw that the several hundred bottles of wine they had prepared had been drunk by the invisible entourages of the two immortals.

# 朝三暮四

原文：

yǐ shù yú rén，yuē zhāo sān mù sì
以术愚人，曰朝三暮四

故事：

战国时期（前475—前221）的哲学家庄子，在他的著作里讲了许多有趣而又意味深长的寓言故事，“朝三暮四”就是其中一个。

这个故事说的是，古时候宋国有个老人，喜欢猴子，就在家里养它们。时间一长，他家里的猴子越来越多，竟然成为一大群。猴子喜欢活动，为了照顾它们，老人花了很多时间。因为整天与猴子在一起，他对这些猴子的习性和脾气了解得很清楚，猴子们发出声音、做出动作，他就能明白猴子们的意思，而猴子们也能听懂他的话。

养这么一大群猴子，每天需要供应很多食物。老人宁愿把家人的食物节省下来，也要满足猴子们的胃口。但是过了一段时间，因为猴子的数量实在太多，家里的食物无论怎样都不够吃了。老人希望限制一下猴子们每天所吃的食物的数量，但他又深知猴子的脾气，担心它们以后不再顺从自己。他跟猴子们商量说："现在家里的食物不多了，今后每天早晨给你们三颗橡子，晚上给四颗，你们觉得够不够？"

以前，每只猴子每天早晨和晚上都能分到四颗橡子。它们听说早上只有三颗橡子，食物减少了，都很生气，又跳又叫地发起脾气来。

老人一看情形不对，赶紧抚慰它们，答应给他们增加食物，猴子们这才安静下来。于是老人宣布："那么，今后每天早上给你们四颗橡子，晚上给三颗，这样就够了吧？"

猴子们一听，早上的橡子由三个又变成了四个，就以为它们所分到的食物增加了。于是它们都高兴地趴在地上，伸出爪子，等待老人给他们分发橡子。

庄子讲这个故事的用意，是揭露老人愚弄猴子的骗术，其实橡子的总数并没有变，只是分配方式有所变化，就使猴子们转怒为喜。他以此告诫人们要注重实际，不要被巧妙的语言所蒙骗。后来人们使用这个成语，也用来批评那些反复无常、经常变卦的人。

# Three in the morning and four in the afternoon

During the Warring States period (475–221 BC), the philosopher Zhuangzi told many interesting fables with profound significance in his works. "Three in the morning and four in the afternoon" is just one of them.

The story goes like this: an elderly man in the ancient Song Kingdom raised monkeys in his family as a hobby. After a period of time, his family had a big group of monkeys. As monkeys liked exercise, the elder spent a lot of time to take care of them properly. Because he spent so much time with the monkeys, the elder clearly understood the habits and temperaments of the monkeys. He could understand what these monkeys wanted by only hearing their voices and seeing their acts, and the monkeys could also understand what he was saying.

A great amount of food was required every day to raise such a big group of monkeys. The elder tried to satisfy the appetite of the monkeys even if his family members suffered from hunger. But after a period of time, the available food in the family was not enough for the monkeys no matter what method was adopted, as the monkey group had gotten so big. The elder want to restrict the quantity of foods eaten by the monkeys every day. But he knew the temperament of the monkeys as well and worried that they would not obey him later on. He then negotiated with the monkeys: "The family does not have enough

food, I can only give you three acorns in the morning and four in the afternoon every day. Is that ok?"

As each monkey previously got four acorns both in the morning and in the afternoon, they turned angry and jumped and cried when hearing that only three acorns were to be provided in the morning.

Seeing this situation, the elder consoled them at once and agreed to increase the food for them. The monkey group then resumed their quietness. The elder declared: "In the future, I will offer four acorns in the morning and three in the afternoon. Is this ok?"

Hearing that the number of acorns provided in the morning had been changed from three to four, the monkeys thought that they would get more food. Therefore, they bent over the ground and stretched out their claws, waiting for the elder's distribution of acorns.

The original purpose for Zhuangzi telling this story is to unearth the elder's deceitful trick. In fact, the total number of acorns did not change and only the method of distribution changed, which makes the monkeys mood change from fury to happiness. He just wanted to tell people to rely on reality and to be cautious of sweet words. Later on, people used this idiom to criticize people who change their ideas constantly.

# 毛遂自荐

原文：

máo suí jī zhòng lù lù wú qí
毛遂讥众，碌碌无奇

máo suí zì jiàn cái qí chǔ náng biàn dāng tuō yǐng
毛遂自荐才奇，处囊便当脱颖

máo suí piàn yán jiǔ dǐng rén zhòng qí yán
毛遂片言九鼎，人重其言

故事：

战国时期，秦国逐渐强大起来，经常对其他国家发动战争。有一次，秦兵围困了赵国的都城。赵国派大臣平原君去向楚国请求救兵。

平原君是当时最有名的政治家之一，在家里供养着门客几千人。他知道这次与楚国谈判不能够失败，就决定挑选二十个既有勇力又有谋略的门客随他一同前往楚国。可是挑来挑去，几千人里竟然只找出十九个符合要求的人，其他人都无法令平原君满意。

这时，有一个叫毛遂的人走上前来，向平原君自我推荐说："我叫毛遂，听说您的随从人员还缺少一个，希望您把我当作那第二十个人。"平原君对他毫无印象，就问："你来到我这儿几年了？"毛遂说："三年了。"平原君说："有才能的人在社会上，就好像一把锥子放在布袋里，它的尖端很快就会露出来。你到我这儿已经三年，周围的人们都没有称赞过你的才能，我也没有听过你的名字。看来你没有什么才能，还是留在赵国吧。"

毛遂说："那是因为我今天才请求您把我放在布袋中。如果我早就处在布袋里面的话，整个锋芒都会露出来，而不仅仅是露出个尖端。"平原君于是同意带毛遂一起去楚国。另外十九个人互相用眼光示意，嘲笑毛遂。但是在前往楚国的路上，毛遂与这些同伴讨论问题，这十九个人都被他说服了。

平原君到了楚国，与楚王反复谈判，从早晨太阳出来就

开始谈，到中午太阳当空时还没有结果。他带来的那十九个人也都没有办法改变这种局面，只好对毛遂说：“还是毛先生上去帮忙吧！”毛遂于是走到谈判桌前，对平原君说：“赵、楚联合的事，两句话就可以决定。这样反复谈判还不能决定，是为什么？”楚王很不高兴，对毛遂说：“还不赶快退下去！我是在同你的主人说话，你算干什么的？”毛遂手握剑柄，说：“大王敢斥责我，是由于楚国人多。但是现在我们离得这么近，楚国人再多也没有用，你的性命掌握在我的手里。我听说，商汤和周文王起初只有很小的地盘，但最后他们都统一了天下。现在楚国的国土很大，军队上百万，却屡次遭到秦军的欺侮。赵国与楚国结盟，对楚国也有好处，并不是只对我们赵国有利。既然我的主人在这儿，为什么您不顾及他的面子，而要斥责我呢？”楚王被毛遂说服，又害怕他真的伤害自己，赶紧同意签定盟约。

平原君完成使命回到赵国，感慨地说：“今后我再也不敢说自己有识别人才的眼光了。毛先生在楚国的表现，大大提高了赵国的威望；毛先生那三寸长的舌头，胜过上百万的军队。而这样的人才，我居然一直没有发现！”于是，他把毛遂作为上等宾客对待。

后人将这个故事概括为一个成语“毛遂自荐”，表示某个人不经过别人的介绍，自我推荐做某件事情。

# Mao Sui Recommends Himself

In the Warring States Period, after the Kingdom of Qin became gradually stronger, it often waged wars on other kingdoms. On one occasion, the Qin army besieged the capital city of the Kingdom of Zhao. King Zhao sent Lord Pingyuan to go to the Kingdom of Chu and ask King Chu to send troops to help Zhao.

Lord Pingyuan, one of the most famous politicians at that time, treated several thousand family retainers generously. Because he realized that this negotiation with the Kingdom of Chu could not fail, Lord Ping Yuan decided to take with him twenty men who were well versed in both the letters and the martial arts. Nevertheless, he could find only nineteen men that were suitable among his family retainers. No one else could make Lord Pingyuan satisfied.

Then Mao Sui came forward to the Lord Pingyuan and recommended himself, "I am Mao Sui. I hear there are only 19 men in your entourage and I hope I can be the 20th." Lord Pingyuan had no impression of him, asking, "How many years have you been here?" Mao Sui replied, "Three years." Lord Pingyuan said, "Such a capable person in a group is like an awl in a cloth bag; the awl will immediately pierce the bag and reveal itself. Since you have been here for three years, people around you have never praised your capabilities and I did not know you at all. It seems that you have no special capabilities, and I advise you to stay at home."

Mao Sui answered, "I am asking you to put me in the bag today! If you had done so before, the awl as a whole would have come through the bag before, instead of the point of the awl!" Lord Pingyuan then took Mao Sui with him to the Kingdom of Chu. Judging from the expressions on the faces of the other 19 envoys, they all mocked Mao Sui. Nevertheless, they were all persuaded by Mao Sui when they discussed issues with him on the way to the Kingdom of Chu.

Lord Pingyuan went to the Kingdom of Chu. He began to negotiate with King Chu from the early morning, however, there was no progress at noon. The 19 envoys had no way to change the situation. They came to Mao Sui, saying, "Mao Sui, please have a try!" Then Mao Sui came to the negotiating table and told his Lord, "Only by using a couple of remarks can we sign an alliance with the Kingdom of Chu. How come we got nowhere after rounds of negotiations and arguments?" King Chu was rather unhappy, telling Mao Sui, "Retreat in a hurry! I am not talking with you but your Lord. You are nothing." With a hand on his sword hilt, Mao Sui said, "Why does King Chu dare to reprimand me? It is because you have a huge army. But the army cannot arrive here if I kill you since we are so close! I hear that King Tang of Shang Dynasty and King Wen of Zhou started with small lands but they finally united the country. Now, the Kingdom of

Chu has a vast territory and millions of troops only to find that your country is often bullied and humiliated by the Kingdom of Qin. The alliance between our two kingdoms is beneficial to both parties. Since my Lord is present, why did you reprimand me in front of him?" King Chu, who was persuaded by Mao Sui and was also afraid of being killed, immediately agreed to sign a treaty with the Kingdom of Zhao.

Lord Pingyuan returned to the Kingdom of Zhao with his mission finished, commenting with emotion, "From now on I do not think I have super vision to identify talents. The performance of Mao Sui in the Kingdom of Chu has greatly enhanced the prestige of our kingdom: He has beaten millions of troops with his sliver tongue and golden wit. However, I did not know him, such a great talent, before!" Since then, he treated Mao Sui with much more respect.

Later, the story was summarized as an idiom, which now can be used whenever a person recommends himself for a job or position.

# 破釜沉舟

原文：

zhì zài bì shèng，yuē pò fǔ chén zhōu
志在必胜，曰破釜沉舟

故事：

秦朝（前221—前206）末年，人们纷纷起来反抗秦的暴政。秦军派出几十万大军，将反秦武装赵国的军队围困在巨鹿城（在今天的河北省）。其他反秦军队纷纷赶来援助，但是看到秦军强大的阵容之后，他们都吓得躲回军营里。人们把希望寄托在南方反秦武装楚国的身上。

楚王任命宋义为统帅，项羽为副将，让他们率领军队增援巨鹿。可是走到半路上，宋义就命令军队停下来，一停就是一个半月。当时天气很冷，下着大雨，士兵们缺少衣服和粮食，又冷又饿。大家都抱怨宋义。项羽是以英勇善战著称的将军，他去找宋义，问为什么不赶快前去救援赵军。宋义说："现在秦军很强大，不如先让赵军与他们战斗，消耗他们的力

量。然后，我们再去攻打秦军，一定可以获胜。披着坚固的铠甲、拿着锐利的武器与敌人拼搏，我比不上您；但坐下来运用谋略，您就不如我了。”他还下命令说，不听从他指挥的人，都要被处死。

项羽对宋义的做法很气愤，对将士们说：“如果秦军打败了赵军，力量会更加强大，我们哪里还能打败他们。我们楚国的命运将由这次行动决定，如今宋义却不敢去攻打秦军。还有，将士们缺少食物，宋义竟然还在大吃大喝。国家不需要这样的人。”于是项羽趁着早晨拜见宋义的机会，将宋义杀死。他假装得到了楚王的命令，对众人说：“宋义想背叛我们楚国，所以楚王暗中命令我处死他。”楚王知道这件事后，只好任命项羽为新的统帅。

取得军队的指挥权之后，项羽立刻带领大军渡过一条大河去救赵国。等军队都过了河，他下令把船只全部凿沉，把军营中用来做饭的锅都打碎，还放火烧掉了全部营房，士兵们身上只带着够吃三天的食物。项羽告诉大家，如果他们失败了，就再也没有退路；大家只有拼死一战，将秦军打败，才能活下去。这就意味着，他们只有三天时间来打败强大的秦军。士兵们听了，都恨不得马上就能与秦军作战。这样，楚军就以最快的速度赶到了巨鹿城下。

项羽指挥楚军与秦军展开激烈的战斗，在他带领下，楚军人人奋勇作战，喊杀声震天动地，每个人都抵得上秦军十个人。其他救援的军队看到这场景，都觉得极其紧张和害怕。经过多次交锋，楚军以少胜多，终于把秦军打得大败而逃。其他救援军的将领去见项羽，都恭敬而又害怕地爬在地上，不敢抬起头来。从此之后，各路反秦的军队都接受项羽的指挥。

成语“破釜沉舟”来自这个历史故事，用来比喻不惜一切代价做某件事的巨大决心和不达目的决不回头的气魄。

# To Break the Cauldrons and Sink the Boats

At the end of the Qin Dynasty (221 BC–206 BC), people rebelled against the tyranny of the Qin one after another. The Kingdom of Qin sent an army, with hundreds of thousands of soldiers, to attack the Kingdom of Zhao and surrounded the Zhao army, one of the armies against Qin, in the city of Julu (now in Hebei province). Other armies against Qin rushed to help the Zhao's army out of trouble. On seeing the strength of the Qin army, they were scared into hiding in their own barracks. People had to place their hopes in the army of southern Chu.

King Chu sent two generals, Song Yi and Xiang Yu, to rescue the army of Zhao, with Song Yi as commander-in-chief and Xiang Yu as deputy commander-in-chief. The two generals led the army north. When they went half way, General Song Yi refused to advance any more. He stayed there for one and a half months. At that time, it was cold. It rained heavily. The soldiers felt cold and hungry lacking clothing and food. They all complained to Song Yi. General Xiang Yu, famous for fighting valiantly and skillfully on battlefields, went to Song Yi and asked him why he decided not to advance farther to rescue the army of Zhao. Song Yi replied, "Now the army of Qin is very powerful, outnumbering our army. Why not let them fight against the army of Zhao first? After the army of Qin weakens its power, we can attack them and we will defeat them. You can beat me by fighting against enemies dressed in strong armor and carrying sharp weapons. However, my strong point is to use strategy, and you must listen to me when it comes to the implementation of strategy." Song Yi also ordered that those who did not obey his command should be executed.

Xiang Yu was angry at Song Yi's decision, telling the soldiers, "If the army of Qin defeats the army of Zhao, it will become more powerful. The chance of beating the army of Qin will be slim. The fate of the Kingdom of Chu will be determined by this battle. However, Song Yi does not dare to fight against the army of Qin right now. Our soldiers lack clothing and food, while Song Yi is still squandering food. Our kingdom does not need such a person." So Xiang Yu killed Song Yi on a morning when he visited Song Li. Xiang Yu pretended to have received the order of the King of Chu, telling the soldiers, "Song Yi wants to betray the Kingdom of Chu, so King Chu secretly ordered me to execute him." Having known the news, King Chu had to appoint Xiang Yu as commander-in-chief.

Immediately, the new commander-in-chief led his troops cross a river to rescue the Kingdom of Zhao. When all the troops had crossed the river, Xiang Yu ordered them to smash all the Cauldrons and sink all the boats, and set fire to all the barracks. The soldiers took only three days' food. Xiang Yu told the soldiers, "If we are defeated, they are sure to die because we cannot retreat. Only by fighting heroically and defeating the army of Qin will we be able to survive!" This means they must defeat the powerful army of Qin within three days. On hearing this, the soldiers were determined to advance and win the battle. As a result, the army of Chu arrived in the city of Julu at the fastest pace.

Under the leadership of Xiang Yu, all the soldiers fought heroically. Almost every one, yelling and screaming, could defeat 10 soldiers

in the army of Qin in fierce fights. Other troops rescuing the army of Zhao felt scared to death on seeing those fierce fights. After several encounters, the army of Chu beat the outnumbered army of Qin. In the end, the army of Qin fled. The commanders-in-chief of other troops rescuing the army of Zhao could not raise their heads because of respect and were scared when they went to see Xiang Yu. Since then, all troops against Qin accepted the leadership of Xiang Yu.

The idiom "to break the cauldrons and sink the boats" was originated from this historical story, which now can be used as a metaphor, describing a person who has great determination and confidence to achieve his goal at all costs.

# 刻舟求剑

原文：

kè zhōu qiú jiàn，gù ér bù tōng
刻舟求剑，固而不通

故事：

楚国是中国历史上春秋战国时代（前770—前221）南方的一个诸侯国，长江穿过楚国，另外楚国境内还有很多河流和湖泊，人们出门时经常要坐船。

有一次，有个楚国人乘船过江，要到江的另一边去。他是个有社会地位的人，随身佩戴着一把样子美观的宝剑。他对这把剑很喜欢，即便是在船上，也拿在手里玩赏。可是他一不小心，将这把宝剑掉进江里去了。

船夫连忙停止划船，想帮助他将这把贵重的剑捞上来，其他乘船的人也纷纷帮着想办法。剑的主人却一点儿也不着急，拿出一把小刀，在船上刻了一个记号，嘴里还说："我的剑是从这儿掉下去的。"人们劝他赶紧到江水里去捞取宝

剑，他却很有把握地说："这里水很深，浪很大，不适合下去找剑。不过我已经做了记号，等船靠岸了再找。还是先走吧。"大家不明白他到底在想什么，于是船就继续向对岸划去。

等到船靠了岸，这个楚国人一看岸边的江水很浅，就脱掉衣服，从船上刻有记号的地方跳下去，想找到他那把漂亮的宝剑。他在水里摸来摸去，当然什么也没找到。他站在水里向人们大声喊："真是奇怪呀，我的剑明明是从这儿掉到江里的，我明明做了记号，可是为什么找不到剑呢？"

船上的其他人这才知道，原来他竟然是这么糊涂的人。大家回头看看，船已经从江的那一边来到了这一边，剑当然不会跟着船跑过来。这个楚国人就这样丢掉了心爱的宝剑。

成语"刻舟求剑"就是从这个故事来的，现在用它来比喻不考虑事物的发展变化、死板地按照教条来行动的做法。

# To Carve a Mark in the Boat and Look for the Sword

During China's Spring and Autumn and Warring States Period (770 BC – 221 BC), the Kingdom of Chu lies in Southern China. People there often go out by boat to cross the Yangtze River and many rivers and lakes inside the kingdom.

There was once a man from the Kingdom of Chu who took a boat to cross the Yangtze river from one end of the Yangtze river. As a man with social status, he always dressed a beautiful sword on hand. He was fond of this sword very much. Even on the boat, he enjoyed beating time with the sword he was carrying in his hand. Nevertheless, the sword fell into the river by accident. The boatman stopped rowing immediately, trying to help him find his treasured sword. Others on the boat also helped him to find solutions. The owner of the sword, however, seemed not anxious at all. He took out a knife and carved a mark in the boat, murmuring, "This is where my sword fell." When people urged him to jump in to find the sword as soon as possible, he said confidently," The water here is very deep. The wave here is very strong. It is unsuitable to bring back my sword from here. Nevertheless, I have made a mark on the side of the boat and I would find the sword when the boat crossed the river. Don't stop moving the boat first." No one understood what he was thinking, and the boat continued to cross the river.

Until the boat arrived at the other side of the river where the water was not so deep, the man took off his dress to find his sword at the place where he had marked. He wanted to find his beautiful sword. He

searched in the river only to find nothing he wanted. He stood in the river, screaming to people around him, "How strange it is! My sword fell into the river just from here, where I had made a mark on the side of the boat. But how come I can't find it?"

Other people on the boat began to realize that the man was so foolish. They knew although the boat had moved, the sword did not move. The man lost his beloved sword in such a foolish way!

The idiom "to carve a mark in the boat and look for the sword" was originated from this story, which now can be used as a metaphor, describing a person who refuses to listen to logic, but stubbornly adheres to his own opinions.

# Legendary Tales
# 传说故事

# 嫦娥奔月

原文：

hòu yì qī，bēn yuè gōng ér wéi cháng é
**后羿妻，奔月宫而为嫦娥**

故事：

古代中国人认为月亮上面有一座华丽的宫殿，里面住着一位美丽的仙女，名叫嫦娥。可是除了一只白兔以外，她没有别的伙伴，非常寂寞。嫦娥怎么会一个人跑到月亮上面去呢？这里有一个流传很广的“嫦娥奔月”的传说。

上古时代尧帝的时候，天上突然同时出现了十个太阳，它们发出的光照在大地上，植物都被晒死了，河里的水被烤干，大地裂开了一道道缝，就连岩石都快要被熔化了。许多凶残的野兽也趁机出来危害人类。人类的生存面临严峻考验。

这时候，一位英雄及时出现了，他就是特别擅长射箭的羿（yì）。羿本来是天上的神，不忍心看人类遭受这样的灾难，所以前来解救。他弯弓搭箭向天上射去，每一箭都射落一个太阳；一连射出九箭，九个太阳都被射落，掉进了东海里面。这样，天上就跟原来一样，只剩下一个太阳。

大旱灾结束了，羿又到处去捕杀那些危害人类的猛兽和怪物，包括长着很长的尖牙、样子像人的怪物，长着九个头的蛇，非常巨大的鸟，还有巨大的野猪。羿勇敢善战，将它们一一杀死。但是，天帝对羿射落九个太阳的行为很不高兴，解除了他的天神身份。羿失去了飞回天上的能力，只好

生活在人间。

羿的妻子就是嫦娥，她本来也是天上的神仙，跟随羿一起来到人间。现在，她和羿一样，也无法重新回到天上去了。羿帮人类除害的时候，她只能独自待在家里；现在羿心情不好，经常一个人跑到外面去打猎，嫦娥仍然独自在家。她觉得很寂寞、痛苦，对羿产生了不满。

羿听说昆仑山上住着一位女神西王母，她拥有一种不死药，吃了之后就可以恢复上天的能力。于是他就到昆仑山去，走了很长的路，历经种种艰难险阻，终于见到了西王母。西王母很同情羿的遭遇，把不死药送给了羿。羿拿着不死药，高高兴兴回到家里，准备选一个合适的日子，与嫦娥一起吃下它，重新回到天上。

可是嫦娥因为对羿很不满，决定离开他独自生活。这一天，她趁羿不在家，偷偷拿出他藏起来的不死药一口吞下。这不死药果然很神奇，吃完之后，嫦娥就飞上了天空，向月亮奔去。

嫦娥来到月亮上面之后，才发现这儿除了她之外没有别人，冷冷清清的。宫殿虽然很大、很漂亮，但一个人住着有什么意思呢？她找来找去，发现月亮上只长着一棵桂花树，还有一只白兔。她很后悔丢下了丈夫一个人来到天上，就和那只白兔每天捣药，希望可以制出神奇的药，再飞回羿的身边。

失去了妻子和不死药的羿，只能继续生活在人间。他收了一个徒弟，指导这个徒弟学射箭。可是这个徒弟心肠歹毒，学到本领之后，就想成为唯一的射箭高手，于是卑鄙地暗杀了羿。这样一来，嫦娥即使造出灵药，也不能见到丈夫了。从此，她独自居住在月亮上，永远承受着孤独和悔恨的折磨，成了一个不快乐的仙女。

# Chang'e Flies to the Moon

Ancient Chinese people believe that there is a magnificent palace called "Moon Palace" in the moon, where a beautiful fairy named Chang'e lives. She is very lonely because she has no companions but a jade rabbit. How does Chang'e fly to the moon alone? The legend Chang'e Flying to the Moon is a popular fable of ancient China.

In the reign of the legendary Emperor Yao, there were ten suns rising in the sky at the same time. The heat from ten suns shining scorched all crops on the land. Rivers dried up, the land became barren, and rocks melted. Beasts were killing humans. The human race was facing a severe challenge to survive.

Then, a legendary hero named Hou Yi, a great archer, appeared in time. He was one of the immortals living in heaven. He came down to earth to solve the problem of the ten suns and end the catastrophe. Hou Yi, using his legendary archery skills, drew his extraordinary bow and shot down the nine superfluous suns one after another, which all fell into the East China Sea. In this way, the sky resumed to normal, leaving only one sun rising and setting according to time.

After the drought ended, Hou Yi went around to kill dangerous and harmful beasts and monsters, including a monster with a long fang and a human face, a nine-headed snake, very large birds, and huge wild boars. Hou Yi killed them one by one in a courageous and skillful way. Nevertheless, the Jade Emperor was obviously not pleased with Hou Yi's solution to save the earth: nine of his sons were dead. As a punishment, the Jade Emperor deprived Hou Yi of his immortal identity. Having lost the ability to fly back to heaven, Hou Yi had to live as a mortal on the earth.

Chang'e, Hou Yi's wife, was also an immortal living in heaven. She descended to earth and became a mortal to accompany her husband. Like Hou Yi, she could not return to heaven, either. When Hou Yi was busy with killing monsters, Chang'e stayed at home alone. When Hou Yi was in a bad mood, he often went hunting outside and left Chang'e alone at home. Gradually, she felt very lonely and painful. Therefore, she began to resent her husband.

After he heard that there lived the Empress Xiwangmu in the Kunlun Mountain, who had a parcel of elixir, by taking which, it was said, one would ascend immediately to the heaven and become a celestial being, Hou Yi decided to journey on a long, perilous quest to get one. When they finally met, the Empress Xiwangmu showed sympathy on his misfortune and gave him the pill. Hou Yi fetched the pill, going home happily. He was ready to select an appropriate day to take the

pill together with his wife, Chang'e, to fly back to heaven.

Nevertheless, Chang'e was angry with Hou Yi at that time. She decided to live alone without him. One day when she was alone at home, she found the elixir, which Hou Yi hid in a secret place, and swallowed it. The elixir did create a miracle: After eating it, Chang'e ascended to the moon.

Chang'e landed on the moon only to find the Moon Palace a cheerless place with no one else living there. The Moon Palace was significant and beautiful, but she found this abode boring. She searched all the abode but only found a cassia tree and a jade rabbit. She regretted leaving her husband and ascending to the heaven without him, so she and the jade rabbit pounded pills every day in the hope to make a magic pill and to fly back to her husband by taking it.

Hou Yi was forced to live on earth after he lost his wife and elixir. He had an apprentice, who was a malicious man by nature. Hou Yi taught him how to learn archery. Nevertheless, the apprentice wanted to be the sole master of archery after he mastered archery. He despicably killed Hou Yi. Since her husband was dead, Chang'e could not meet him forever even if she could manufacture a cure. Since then, she has been living in the Moon Palace alone. She has to suffer loneliness and regret forever and become an unhappy fairy.

# 夸父追日

原文：

shì bú liàng lì，bù shū kuā fù zhuī rì
事不量力，不殊夸父追日

故事：

传说远古时候，在北方荒野中生活着一群巨人，他们住在一座高山上。他们的首领名叫夸父。夸父喜欢玩蛇，他每只耳朵上各挂着一条黄蛇，双手也各挥舞着一条黄蛇。夸父身材高大，矫健敏捷，奔跑起来像飞鸟一样，谁也跑不过他。

夸父和他的族人们生活的环境很恶劣，经常面临各种猛兽和自然灾害的威胁。北方天气寒冷，太阳每天从东方升起，人们还没有充分享受它带来的光明和温暖，它又急匆匆地奔向西方了。夸父望着在天空中运行的太阳，决定去追赶它，让它按自己族人的愿望来运行。族人们担心夸父追不上太阳，但夸父对自己的奔跑速度很有信心，决心与太阳比个高下。

打定主意后，夸父马上开始行动。太阳化身为三条腿的神鸟，飞过天空，向西方极其遥远的地方飞去。夸父也迈开大步，迅速向西追赶。太阳在天空中飞行，夸父则在地上飞奔，他奔跑的速度与太阳飞行的速度不相上下。追赶了整整一天，傍晚时分，当太阳缓缓落在它休息的地方的时候，夸父也赶到了这里。看着近在眼前的巨大的太阳，夸父非常兴奋，他赶紧跑上前去，想抓住太阳。

可是夸父没有想到，太阳就像一座燃烧的熔炉，一下子就把他身上的水分都烤干了。夸父感到特别口渴，只好离开太阳，掉头奔向黄河。他跑到这条中国古人心目中的第一大河旁边，急不可待地畅饮河水。夸父的身躯非常庞大，转眼之间，滔滔奔流的黄河变得平静下来，水流越来越小，原来夸父竟然一口气喝干了全部的黄河水。但是，他仍然觉得很渴，只好又跑到渭（wèi）河边上。渭河是黄河的一条支流，夸父一阵狂饮，这条河水也马上干涸了。夸父仍然感到干渴得难以忍受，就奔向极其遥远的北方，那儿有个大湖，非常宽阔，方圆几千里，全世界的飞禽都到那里繁衍后代，更换羽毛。大湖里的水，应该能够消除夸父的焦渴。但是，大湖的距离太远了，夸父还没有跑到那里，体力就已经耗尽。他最终没能到达大湖，又渴又累，在半路上就倒下了。这位勇敢地与太阳赛跑的英雄，就这样悲壮地死去了。临死前，他把手杖扔出去，手杖落在地上，变成了一大片郁郁葱葱的桃树林。

夸父的族人知道这片桃树林是夸父留给他们的，就在桃树林的西边建立了一个国家，名字就叫夸父国。夸父国的人都继承了夸父的高大身材和勇敢精神。

# Kua Fu Chases the Sun

In ancient times, there lived a group of mighty giants on a mountain in the northern forests and Kua Fu was their leader. Kua Fu kept the ferocious snakes he caught on his ears for decoration, or held them in his hands waving proudly. He was a person with extraordinary physical power. He ran faster than anyone else and he could run as fast as flying birds.

At that time, Kua Fu and other mighty giants lived in a desolate and uncultured world, infested with vipers and beasts. It was chilly in the north. The sun rose in the east every day, but ran west at a fast pace, leaving people with a limited time to enjoy its light and warmth. Looking at the running sun in the sky, Kua Fu decided to catch up with it and tame it to serve all people in his own tribe. Others were worried that Kua Fun would fail to catch up with the sun, but Kua Fun was so confident in his running ability that he decided to try chasing the sun.

Once he made the decision, Kua Fu immediately started. The sun, transforming itself into a three-legged divine bird, flew across the sky and towards the remote west. Kua Fu chased the sun with flying strides. The sun moved fleetingly in the sky, while Kua Fu chased it like wind on the ground. What a good match between them! After chasing a whole day, when the evening was coming, the sun slowly fell to its setting place and Kua Fu followed the sun there. With the huge sun so close, Kua Fu was very excited. He quickly ran to the sun and wanted to seize it.

Nevertheless, when he was near the burning sun, it immediately dried up all the water in his body, which he never took into account.

Kua Fu felt extremely thirsty. He couldn't stand it anymore so he rushed to the Yellow River, the longest river of the ancient Chinese, and drank water from the river. With all the surging torrents becoming calm and currents becoming smaller and smaller, the river was drunken up by Kua Fu, a giant with a large skeleton, all at once. Feeling still very thirsty, he went to the Weihe River, a tributary of the Yellow River, and drank up this river too. But he still felt horribly thirsty, so he rushed to the north where there was a big lake. The lake, covering several thousand miles, was said to be such a place where all the birds around the world gave birth and grow new feathers. The water from the big lake should have been sufficient to satisfy him. However, it was too far away and he died of thirst and exhaustion on the way. In this way, the brave hero chasing the sun died in a tragic way. Before dying, he threw his stick out. Immediately the stick dropped to the ground, it turned into a large lush peach forest.

The people of Kua Fu's tribe founded a country at the west of the peach forest that Kua Fu left to them. They inherited Kua Fu's tall stature and brave heart.

# 牛郎织女

原文：

niú nǚ liǎng xiù， wéi qī xī yì xiāng féng
牛女两宿，惟七夕一相逢

qī xī niú nǚ dù hé， jiā jiā chuān qǐ qiǎo zhī zhēn
七夕牛女渡河，家家穿乞巧之针

jià què qiáo yǐ dù hé， niú nǚ xiāng huì
架鹊桥以渡河，牛女相会

故事：

中国人很早就注意到，天上有两颗肉眼可以清楚地看到的恒星，一颗在银河的东边，一颗在银河的西边，遥遥相对。中国人把这两颗星星分别称为牵牛星和织女星。再后来，人们认为这两颗恒星是一对夫妇变成的，这就是民间广泛流传的牛郎织女故事。

相传在古时候，有兄弟两个人，他们的父母早早就去世了。哥哥和嫂子对弟弟不好，两个人分家时。哥哥霸占了所有的田地和房屋，而弟弟只得到一头黄牛。弟弟每天细心地照顾牛，带着牛帮别人干活来维持生活，所以人们都叫他牛郎。

一天，这头黄牛忽然像人那样说起话来，它告诉牛郎，农历七月初七那天的晚上，天上的仙女们会到人间来，如果能偷走一位仙女的衣服，就能和她结婚。这天晚上，牛郎按照黄牛的指点，悄悄来到湖边，躲在草丛里。不久，天上宫殿的大门打开，飞出七个美丽的仙女。她们飞到湖边，脱了衣服下去洗澡，并在湖水里快乐地嬉戏。牛郎趁她们不注意，偷了一件衣服藏起来。

仙女们洗完了澡，上岸穿好衣服，纷纷飞回天宫里去。但是，年龄最小的仙女找不到自己的衣服，因此无法飞走，

急得哭了起来。这时牛郎赶紧出来，将衣服还给她。原来，这个仙女是天帝的第七个女儿，心灵手巧，天上美丽的云彩就是由她织出来的，所以她的名字叫织女。经过交谈，织女认为牛郎是一个勤劳而善良的人，就同意和他结婚。织女和牛郎一起生活，夫妻两人非常恩爱，牛郎带着黄牛去干活儿，织女就在家里织布、做饭。后来，他们又生了一个儿子和一个女儿，一家四口人过着幸福美满的生活。

天宫里面，因为织女没有回来，就没有人去织造云彩了。天帝和他的妻子王母娘娘派人到处寻找织女，当他们知道织女嫁给了人间的小伙子牛郎之后，非常生气。天帝派天兵天将到人间来，把织女抓回天宫。牛郎在黄牛的帮助下，也拥有了上天的能力，他把儿女装在两个筐子里，挑着他们，上天去追赶织女。王母娘娘不想让这对夫妻再见面，看到牛郎快要追上织女了，她就拔下头上的银钗，在他们中间划了一下；这一划，天空中就出现了一条宽阔的银河，挡在牛郎、织女之间。从此以后，夫妻二人只能流着眼泪，隔着银河远远地眺望对方。这对痛苦的年轻人就这样变成了银河两边的牵牛星和织女星。

善良的人们和动物们都很同情牛郎、织女。七月初七晚上，许多喜鹊主动飞到银河上，用它们的身体搭成一座跨越银河的桥梁。牛郎、织女走到鹊桥中央，终于又相见了。他们之间坚贞不变的爱情，让天帝也觉得没办法，只好允许他们每年七月初七聚会一次。在中国古代，这一天是女孩子们最重视的节日，在这天她们会举行一些活动，祈求获得织女那样灵巧的手艺和幸福生活。

# The Cowherd and the Weaving Maid

The Chinese people have noticed that there are two stars that are quite visible to the unaided eye in the sky. One is east of the Milky Way, and another is in the west, the two of which stand opposite each other at a distance. They are known as the stars Altair and Vega. They believed that these two stars are a couple. The legend of Niulang, the cowherd, and Zhinü, the Weaving Maid, is widely spread among the Chinese people.

As ancient Chinese legend has it, an orphaned cowherd was mistreated by his elder brother and sister-in-law, who eventually gave him an old ox and chased him out. The cowherd took good care of the old ox and made a living relying on this ox. Therefore, people called him cowherd.

One day the ox suddenly opened its mouth and started talking, telling the cowherd that the heavenly fairies would come to the earth on the evening of the seventh day of the seventh lunar month, and that if he could steal clothes from one of the seven fairies, he could marry her. On that night the cowherd came to the lakeside quietly and hid behind the reeds, waiting for the girls to bathe. Soon after, seven pretty fairies flew to the riverside and went to bathe in the river, playing happily in the water. The cowherd grabbed the Weaving Maid's clothing while they were not looking.

After bathing, all of the other girls but the Weaving Maid got dressed and went back to the heavens, but the youngest of the seven daughters of the Queen of Heaven could not find her clothes and fly away, so she cried anxiously. The cowherd appeared just then and gave back her clothes. He learned that the girl was the seventh daughter of the Queen of Heaven, who was called Weaving Maid because she is excelled at weaving beautiful clouds. After a conversation, the Weaving Maid thought the cowherd was an industrious and virtuous man, so she agreed to marry him.

The cowherd and the Weaving Maid lived happily together and they eventually had two children, a son and a daughter. They led a happy life as the cowherd worked outside the home with his ox and the Weaving Maid weaved at home everyday.

Due to Weaving Maid's absence, no one was able to weave clouds. So the Jade Emperor and his wife, the Queen of Heaven, sent people to search for the Weaving Maid; they were very annoyed when they learned that the Weaving Maid had married an earthly cowherd. They had the Weaving Maid brought back to the heaven. With the help of the cowhide from his loyal ox, the cowherd was able to follow the

Weaving Maid into heaven, bringing his two children along in baskets slung from a carrying pole across his shoulders. He was about to reach his wife when the Queen of Heaven showed up and pulled out her hairpin to separate the two. The line became the Silver River in heaven, or the Milky Way. From then on the couple could only see each other remotely through in tears across the river. The bitter lovers thus became the cowherd Altair and the Weaving Maid Vega.

All men of good will showed great sympathy for the cowherd and Weaving Maid. On the evening of the seventh day of the seventh month, millions of magpies fly up and form a bridge across the Silver River, allowing the couple to meet each other at the center of the bridge. The Jade Emperor was finally moved by their faithful love, so he permitted the couple to meet once every year on the Silver River on the double seventh day. In ancient China, this day is the most important day for maidens. They will have some activities on this day in the hope of getting the clever fingers and happy life as the Weaving Maid.

# 精卫填海

原文：

jīng wèi xián shí, bǐ rén zhī tú láo
精卫衔石，比人之徒劳

故事：

中国神话传说中，南方天帝炎帝有很多后代。他最小的女儿名叫女娃，活泼可爱。女娃喜欢到处玩耍，有一次她独自跑到东海去，不幸遇到了巨大的风浪。女娃苦苦挣扎，最后还是被大海吞没了，再也不能回到父亲身边。

女娃不甘心就这样悲惨地死去。她死后，灵魂变成了一只小鸟。因为这只小鸟总是"精卫、精卫"地叫着，人们就称它为精卫。精卫的样子有点像乌鸦，但是头上有美丽的花纹，还长着白色的喙（huì）和红色的爪子。

精卫痛恨夺去了自己年轻生命的东海，它发誓要向东海报仇。它住在西方的一座山上，离东海很远。每天，它从山上衔一块小石子或是一根小树枝，然后飞很远的距离，将它

们投到东海里去。石子和树枝投到浩瀚的海上，立刻消失得无影无踪，对大海根本没什么影响。海洋里的神听说这只小鸟想要把东海填平，觉得很好笑，因为精卫那样弱小，而东海则如此浩瀚无垠。他劝告精卫停止这种行为，但是精卫不肯放弃，因为它坚信，只要不停地将石子和树枝投进东海，那么总有一天，能够将东海填平。

就这样，精卫不顾劳累，不惧风雨，日复一日地坚持这种复仇的行动。由于每天飞往东海，精卫结识了海燕。它们结为夫妻，生育了很多后代。它们生下的孩子，雌鸟的样子都像精卫，而雄鸟的样子则像海燕。精卫的后代继续每天衔着石子和树枝飞往东海，世世代代都不停止。

# Jingwei is Determined to Fill up the Sea

According to Chinese myths and legends, the Emperor Yan has many descendants. His youngest daughter was named Nüwa, a lively and lovely girl. One day, Nüwa was rowing a small boat by herself toward the East Sea. Unfortunately, a sea storm came and mountain-like waves capsized the small boat. Nüwa lost her life to the merciless sea and could not go back to her father's side.

After she died, Nüwa turned into a bird with red claws and a white beak, vowing to fill up the sea. She was not reconciled to die, she cried the sound of "Jingwei, Jingwei…". She swore vengeance against the East Sea. The bird lived on a mountain near the sea. It hated the sea so much that it decided to fill it up. Every day, it flew to and fro between the mountain and the sea, carrying a twig or a pebble from the mountain and dropping it into the sea. However, the twig and pebble disappeared without a trace after being thrown into the vast sea, and had little influence on the sea. The God of Sea felt it was very funny when he heard this little bird want to fill and level up the East Sea because Jingwei is so small and the East Sea is so vast. He tried to persuade the Jingwei to stop her work, but Jingwei didn't give up. She firmly believed that she could fill up the sea one day as long as she continued to throw twigs and pebbles into the sea unceasingly. She kept filling up the sea unceasingly year after year.

Jingwei spared no effort and insisted on such act of vengeance day after day. Later on, a salangane came across Jingwei while flying over the East Sea. They got married and had many children. All the girls look like their mother and boys look like their father. The descendants of Jingwei continue to hold stones and tree branches with their beaks and throw them into the sea, back and forth, never-ending.

# 屈原与端午节

原文：

duān yáng jìng dù, diào qū yuán zhī nì shuǐ
端阳竞渡，吊屈原之溺水

故事：

每年的农历五月初五是中国的端午节，这个节日与春节、清明节、中秋节一样，都是中国重要的传统节日。在这天，人们吃粽子，喝药酒，还举行龙舟竞赛、游行祭祀等活动。中国人为什么要过这样一个节日呢？据说，这是为了纪念战国时期的伟大诗人屈原。

屈原出生于楚国的一个贵族家庭。当他出生时，楚国已经是一个拥有七百多年历史的古老国家。当时，包括南方的楚国在内，中国有七个诸侯国，他们之间不断发生战争，给人民带来很大灾难。西方的秦国实力强大，也最有野心，想要统一其他六国。屈原深爱自己的祖国，希望楚国能避免灭亡的命运。他博学多才，擅长辩论和外交，楚王很赏识他，让他担任重要的职务。屈原劝说楚王采取了很多措施，任用

有才能的人，爱护百姓，发展经济，增强国家实力。他不辞辛劳地奔走于各国之间，经过他的努力，楚国与其他五国结成了六国联盟，楚王成为联盟的领袖。

秦国一直想破坏六国之间的关系，他们找到了对屈原充满怨恨的一批楚国贵族，包括王后和最高行政长官。这些人接受了秦国的贿赂，不断说屈原的坏话，于是楚王不再信任屈原，屈原被迫离开都城。秦国得知这一情况后，马上派人来楚国，声称愿意送给楚国很多土地，但要求楚国断绝与其他国家的外交关系。贪婪而愚蠢的楚王这样做了，却发现秦国根本不想送土地给他。受了欺骗的楚王愤怒地率兵攻打秦国，大败而归，其他国家也都不帮助楚国。楚王仍不死心，决定亲自到秦国去谈判。屈原听到这个消息后，担心秦王不怀好意，赶紧从远处赶回来劝阻楚王，但楚王没有听他的劝告，还是去了秦国。果然，楚王一到秦国就被囚禁起来。

消息传来，王后等人拥护太子接任王位。屈原再一次冒险赶回京城，想劝说新王恢复六国联盟，迫使秦国释放原来的楚王。但这时掌权的都是当初赶走他的那些贵族，在他们的建议下，新王不但不接受屈原的意见，还把他流放到了遥远的地方。

过了三年，传出原来的楚王去世的消息。这件事使屈原受到沉重打击，他在遥远的南方日夜担忧，害怕楚国遭到更大的灾难。但他不愿意为了逃避灾难而离开楚国。后来，坏消息终于传来，秦国的大军进攻楚国，攻占了楚国的都城，楚国眼看就要灭亡。屈原感到十分痛苦和绝望，就在这一年的五月初五那天，跳进汨（mì）罗江自杀了。

远近的人民听说他们敬爱的大臣和诗人屈原投江自杀，纷纷来到江上，寻找他的遗体。人们用糯米和其他材料做成粽子，扔到江水中，希望水里的动物们吃下这些东西，就不会吃屈原的身体了。还有人把药酒倒入江中，想让水中的动物昏迷，以阻止它们伤害屈原。人们划着船在江上寻找，虽然一直找不到屈原，但他们仍然久久不肯离去。这就是龙舟竞赛的起源。

以后每到五月初五，人们都要划着龙舟到江上投粽子，倾倒药酒，并举行各种活动纪念屈原，端午节的风俗就这样流传下来了。

# Qu Yuan and the Dragon Boat Festival

In China, the fifth day of the fifth lunar month is the Chinese Dragon Boat Festival. Like the Spring Festival, Tomb-Sweeping Day and Mid-autumn Festival, they are all important traditional festivals of Chinese people. On this day, people eat rice dumplings, drink medicated wine and hold dragon boat races and other ritual activities in the memory of Qu Yuan, a famous Chinese poet during the Warring States Period (about 270 B.C.) in ancient China.

Qu Yuan was born in a noble family of the state of Chu which was a powerful nation at that time with more than seven hundred years of history. At that time,. China had seven states including the state of Chu in the south. Consequently, wars constantly broke out amongst these states, which brought great disaster and misfortune to people's lives. The state of Qin was gradually emerging to become the most powerful state in the west of China and revealed ambitions to unify the other six states under its' rule. Qu Yuan was very loyal to Chu, and eager to maintain the Chu state's sovereignty. He won the trust and favor of King Huai for his eloquence and diplomatic ability, and was appointed a high position. He advocated many effective policies and measures, for example, appointing those with talents to positions of authority, caring for the people, developing the economy, and strengthening the country's military strength. Through these efforts, Chu made an alliance with five other states and became a leader of the alliance as a wealthy, prosperous, and prestigious state.

The state of Qin schemed to break up relationships of the other six countries. Some of the noblemen, including the queen and the highest-level magistrates of Chu accepted bribes from the Qin and slandered Qu Yuan. Thus King Huai of Chu lost faith in Qu Yuan and banished him. Knowing this, the king of Qin sent envoys to tempt King Huai of Chu with a large piece of land but only if King Huai of Chu promised to sever diplomatic relations with other countries. The greedy and stupid King of Chu agreed to this. But he was deceived. King Huai was so enraged that he launched two wars against Qin. Each time Chu was defeated, and other states also turned their back on Chu. But King Huai of Chu wouldn't give up and decided to personally go to the state of Qin to hold talks with the king of Qin. Qu Yuan came back to Chu from a distance to discourage the King of Chu when he heard this news, but the king rejected his advice and went to the state of Qin. As expected, King Chu was captured and imprisoned as soon as he set foot on the soil of Qin. The queen and other ministers supported the prince to succeed him when this news came. Qu Yuan came back to the Chu capital again trying to persuade the new king to resume the alliance relations with the other states and force the king of Qin to release King Huai of Chu. However, the state of Chu at that time was actually in the hands of those noblemen who had slandered Qu Yuan and banished him. At their suggestion, the new king ignored Qu Yuan's advice, and exiled him again to a remote place.

Three years later, King Huai of Chu died in the state of Qin, which hit Qu Yuan hard. He worried about the fate of his state day and night in the remote southern region, and feared that the state of Chu may suffer a greater blow one day. But he was unwilling to leave Chu to escape the destruction. After Chu was occupied by the army of the state of Qin, Qu Yuan, out of extreme grief, committed suicide by jumping into the Miluo River on the fifth day of the fifth lunar month.

Popular legend has it that villagers looked for the remains of Qu Yuan and threw rice dumplings (Zongzi) made of sticky rice and other materials into the river in the hope of keeping fish and evil spirits in the water away from his body. Someone poured medicated wine into the river to drug the animal in the water so as to prevent them from hurting his body. People looked for his body from boats on the river. Although they could not find Qu Yuan's body, they were reluctant to leave for a long time. This is the source of dragon boat racing.

The act of racing to search for his body in boats gradually became

the tradition, of dragon boat races held on the fifth day of the fifth lunar month. People will throw Zongzi and pour medicated wine into the river and held various activities to commemorate Qu Yuan, thus the custom of Dragon Boat Festival has come down from generation to generation.

# 桓景重阳避灾

原文：

chóng jiǔ dēng gāo，xiào huán jǐng zhī bì zāi
重九登高，效桓景之避灾

故事：

每年农历九月初九，是中国另外一个传统节日，称为重阳节。每到这一天，民间有登高、赏菊花等习俗。和很多其他传统节日一样，关于重阳节，也有一个古老的传说。

相传在东汉时期，汝南（在现在的河南省上蔡县）地方有个人叫桓（huán）景。当地每年都有瘟疫发作，经常有人和家畜受到瘟疫的侵害而死。桓景决心找到对付瘟疫的办法，就跑去向著名的法师费长房学习法术。费长房从前是个市场管理员，后来跟一个卖药的老人学习法术，老人带着他跳进一个壶里，那里面是个很大的奇异世界。费长房随老人在壶里学了十多天，临走时老人送给他一根竹杖，他骑着竹杖返回家乡，发现竟然已过了十多年，而那根竹杖则变成了一条龙飞走了。从此，费长房就拥有了高明的法术，特别擅长治病和驱逐带来瘟疫的妖魔，可以让人起死回生。

桓景跟着费长房学习，有一天费长房突然对他说："本地流行的瘟疫，是由一个特别厉害的妖魔带来的。九月九日那天，它将侵害你们家那一带，给你们家带来大灾难。现在我也没有办法驱逐它，但可以教你怎么样躲避它。你赶快回去救你的家人吧！记住，那天你们要用红布缝成小袋子，装上一袋茱萸（zhū yú）带在身边；然后登上高山，喝一些菊

花酒，就可以躲开灾祸了。”这时离九月九日已经很近了，桓景连忙往家赶。

九月九日这天，桓景按照费长房的指点，带领家人和邻居登上了附近的一座山。大家都在手臂上系着一个红色布袋，里面装满了茱萸。茱萸是一种可以做中药的植物，有强烈的气味。他们又把准备好的菊花酒喝下去，这种酒也带有奇特的香气。大家在山上待了一天，并没有发生什么事。但是等他们晚上下山回到家里时，惊讶地发现家里养的牛、羊、狗、鸡这些家畜家禽都死掉了。

桓景去向费长房汇报这件事，对他的救命之恩表示感谢。费长房听后叹息说：“那些茱萸和菊花酒使妖魔不能接近你们、伤害你们，所以它就把这些家畜家禽当作你们的替代品杀死了。”经过这次事件后，桓景更加努力地学习，希望早日找出彻底驱逐瘟疫的办法。

后来，远近的人们听说这件事后，也都模仿桓景等人的做法，在九月九日这天登上高处，喝菊花酒，妇女们手臂上系着装茱萸的袋子。这就形成了过重阳节的习俗。在中国古代，很多文学家都写过以重阳节为题材的作品。另外，在中国古代人眼里，两个九还代表健康长寿的意思，所以这个节日又被当作敬重和祝福老人的节日。

# Huan Jing Escapes from Disaster on the Double Ninth Festival

On the ninth day of the ninth lunar month, it is another important traditional festival of China, known as Chongyang Festival, also known as the Double Ninth Festival.

People have the custom of climbing mountains and enjoy chrysanthemums on this day. Like many other important festivals, there is an old story about the Double Ninth Festival.

It is said that in the Eastern Han Dynasty (25 BC–220 AD), there lived a man named Huan Jing in Runan (present-day Shangcai County in Henan Province). The pestilence was prevailing every year in the county. Many villagers and domestic animals died of the disease frequently. Huan Jing was determined to find means to fight this disease. So he started to study magic arts under Fei Changfang, who was resourceful enough to drive all devils away. Fei Changfang formerly was a local market regulator who had learned magic from an old man who sold drugs. The elder took Fei Changfang to jump in a big pot, within it was a big and fantastic world. Fei Changfang learned the magic arts from the elder in the pot for more than ten days. The old man gave him a bamboo cane at the time of his departure, and he drove the bamboo cane to go back to his hometown. Surprisingly, he found that more than ten years had passed, and that bamboo cane changed to a dragon flying away. Since then, Fei Changfang had skillful magic arts, and was excellent in treating illnesses and driving off evil spirits that brought plagues, even bringing the dying back to life.

One day, Fei Changfang told Huan Jing that the prevalent plague in his hometown was brought by a powerful demon, and a terrible disaster would happen to his family on the Double Ninth day. He had no idea to banish it at that moment, but he taught Huan Jing how to avoid bad luck. He told Huan Jing to make a red bag for each one of his family members and put a spray of dogwood in every one. Then leave home quickly and climb to the top of a mountain, most importantly, drink some chrysanthemum wine. Only by doing so can your family avoid this disaster.

On hearing this, Huan Jing rushed home and asked his family to do exactly as his teacher said. Everyone tied a red bag to their arms with sprigs of dogwood in every bag. The dogwood is a plant with a strong fragrance, and is often used as a Chinese herbal medicine. They also drunk some chrysanthemum wine. The whole family climbed a nearby mountain and did not return until the evening. When they got back home, they found all their animals dead, including chickens, sheep, dogs and even the ox. Later Huan Jing told his teacher, Fei Changfang,

about this and expressed his thanks. Fei said that the dogwood and chrysanthemum wine could ward off the evil spirits and the poultry and livestock died in place of Huan Jing's family. After this incident, Huan Jing studied even harder about how to completely cope with the plague.

Since then, when the people came from far and near heard this, they all imitated the behavior of Huan Jing. And so it happened that climbing a mountain, carrying a spray of dogwood and drinking chrysanthemum wine became the traditional activities of the Chongyang Festival. In ancient China, lots of writers created works about the Chongyang Festival. Since nine is the highest odd digit, people take two of them together to signify longevity. Therefore, the Double Ninth Festival has become a special day for people to pay their respects to the elderly.

# Historical Tales

# 历史故事

# 海不扬波

原文：

hǎi bù yáng bō，zhī zhōng guó yǒu shèng rén
海不扬波，知中国有圣人
dōng zhēng pò fǔ，zhōu gōng dà yì miè qīn
东征破斧，周公大义灭亲
zhōu gōng wò fà ér dài shì
周公握发而待士
zhōu gōng dú zhì lǐ yuè
周公独制礼乐

故事：

周朝（前1046—前256）建立两年之后，周武王就去世了。他的儿子周成王即位，只有十来岁，就由周成王的叔叔周公和召（shào）公代理朝政。在周取代商（前1600—前1046）的过程中，周公是周武王的重要助手，武王讨伐商纣王的宣言，就是由周公写的。

当时周朝刚刚建立，面临的问题很多。周公勤奋地处理政事，每天要会见许多人。古代的男人都留着很长的头发，

有时候他正在洗头发，有人来找他，他连忙用手握着湿头发就跑出来，谈完事情回去接着洗，反复好几次才能洗完。有时候他正吃着饭，也有人来求见，他不等嚼完就把饭吐出来，急着去见客人，生怕错过了什么人才。

但这时周朝内部发生了矛盾，因为周公声望很高，武王的另外两个弟弟心中不服，就散布流言蜚语，说周公将做出对不起成王的事，连召公听了这种流言，也对周公有点怀疑。不久，武王那两个弟弟和商纣（zhòu）王的儿子一起发动了叛乱，一些诸侯国也纷纷响应。周公找到姜太公和召公，说他之所以不避嫌疑全面代理朝政，是因为武王死得太早，而成王太年轻，担心好不容易才建立的周朝被推翻。在得到大臣们的支持后，他率兵去讨伐叛军，经过三年苦战，周公终于平定了叛乱，并且使周的势力扩展到东方的海边。

周公平叛以后，没来得及休整，马上投入新的工作。他主持建成了新的国都洛邑(在现在的河南省洛阳市)，召集天下诸侯举行盛大庆典，并且制定了各种典章制度。这些典章制度后来受到孔子等人的赞美。

周公代理朝政六年，将国家治理得非常好，天下太平，人民安乐。邻国都很敬仰周朝，纷纷使派者来拜见成王和周公。此时成王已经长大成人，周公决定把权力交还给他。这个时候，发生了一件有意思的事。

在中国南边很远的海外，有一个国家叫越裳，也派了使者来到周朝进献礼物。这个国家离周朝很远，语言和文化很不相同，无法直接沟通，要经过好几次语言翻译，双方才能明白对方的意思。他们献上珍贵的白雉（zhì）鸡等礼物，成王请他们交给周公，周公说："我们并没有恩德加给贵国，也没有把我们的政令推行到贵国，哪敢把你们当臣属看待，接受这么贵重的礼物呢?"使者通过翻译说："我国的老人们都说：'现在很久都没有发生大风和暴雨等灾难，三年来大海一直风平浪静，我们猜想中国大概是出了伟大的圣人，应该去朝贺。'就这样，我们不远万里来到这里。"越裳国的使者回去的路上迷失了方向，周公特地赐给他们一辆指南车，并派人当向导，送他们回去。

周公将权力移交给成王，自己则恢复大臣的身份。他不忘自己的职责，继续完善各种典章制度。周成王遵从周公的教导，成为贤明的君主；在他的治理下，社会安定，人民和睦，后人认为这个时期是太平盛世。

# The Sea is Calm

King Wu of Zhou (the first king of Zhou, ca. 1050 BC) died two years after the Zhou Dynasty (1046 BC–256 BC) was founded, and so his son succeeded to the crown when he was a teenager, known as King Cheng of Zhou. As the new king was so young, Zhougong (the Duke of Zhou) and Shaogong (Duke of Shao) worked together as regents and supervised government affairs for several years. Between 1600 BC and 1046 BC before the Zhou Dynasty replaced the Shang Dynasty, the Duke of Zhou was an important assistant of King Wu of Zhou, who wrote the declaration that King Wu sent a punitive expedition against despotic Ruler Zhou.

The Zhou Dynasty faced many issues when it was originally established. Zhougong remained active in running government affairs and met many people every day. Chinese men had long hair in the ancient times. Sometimes, when he was washing his hair, somebody wanted to meet him, he ran out promptly to receive the visitor holding his long wet hair, and continued to wash his hair after talking with visitors, so he may finish washing his hair over and over again. Sometimes, when he was eating, a visitor inquired for him, he would spit it out and hurry to meet the guest for fear he might miss some talented person.

However, contradictions occurred in the Zhou Dynasty. Because the prestige of Zhougong was very high, the other brothers of King Wu of Zhou were not convinced and spread a rumor that Zhougong made King Cheng of Zhou sorry. Even Shaogong doubted about him. Soon after, the two brothers of King Wu and a son of King Zhou of Shang Dynasty raised a revolt, some states also responded to this revolt one after another. Zhougong told Jiang Taigong and Shaogong that the reason why he comprehensively dealt with government affairs making light of suspicion was that because he worried that the Zhou Dynasty would be overthrown for the King Cheng of Zhou was too young. After gaining supports from ministers, he led the army to crusade against rebel army. After three years' hard struggle, Zhougong finally put down the rebellion, and made the power of Zhou Dynasty extend to the seaside of east. He immediately threw himself into the new work without taking a short break. He established a new capital Luoyi (present-day Luoyang City, Henan Province), convened other states to hold grand celebrations, and drew up various decrees and regulations, which were praised by Confucius and other scholars.

The Zhou Dynasty was well administered under the control of Zhougong for six years. It was peaceful people enjoyed happiness. The bordering countries all worshiped the Zhou Dynasty, and sent envoys to pay a formal visit to King Cheng of Zhou and Zhougong. At that moment, the King Cheng of Zhou had grown up, so Zhougong decided to hand back the power to the King Cheng.

An interesting thing occurred at that moment. A country called Yueshang located at the remote south of China sent a envoy to offer presents for the Zhou Dynasty. This state was far away from the Zhou

Dynasty. Its language and culture were quite different from the Zhou Dynasty, so the two sides could only understand their counterpart after translations on several occasions. They presented the precious Hakuchi and other gifts to the King Cheng. The King Cheng of Zhou gave them to Zhougong. Zhougong said, "We didn't oblige kindness to your state, and carry out our government orders to your state, how dare we treat you as our subject and accept such precious gifts?" The envoy answered through an interpreter, "The aged of our state said: 'no windstorm and rainstorm and other disasters occur for a long time, and the sea has been clam for three years, a great man must appear in China, so we should worship you.' And that's the reason why we come a thousand miles to meet you." The envoy of Yueshang became lost on his way back. Zhougong bestowed them a southward pointing cart and sent a person to guide him and send him back.

Zhougong transferred his power to the King Cheng and resumed his status as a subject. He never neglected his duty and continued to improve various kinds of decrees and regulations. The King Cheng followed the instructions of Zhougong and became a wise king; under his control, the society was stable and people lived in unity. Therefore, this period is called the millennium by the posterity.

# 廉颇与蔺相如

原文：

wěn jǐng jiāo，xiàng rú yǔ lián pō
刎颈交，相如与廉颇

nù fà bīng guān，lìn xiàng rú zhī yīng qì bó bó
怒发冰冠，蔺相如之英气勃勃

lián pō xiān guó nàn ér hòu sī chóu
廉颇先国难而后私仇

xiàng rú zhōng yǒng，néng shǐ qín tíng guī bì
相如忠勇，能使秦廷归璧

lián pō fù jīng yǐ qǐng zuì，shàn néng huǐ guò
廉颇负荆以请罪，善能悔过

故事：

在中国古代的战国时期，赵国有一位优秀的将领廉颇，以勇猛善战而闻名，立了许多功劳，赵王对他很器重。与廉颇同时代的蔺（lìn）相如这时地位很低微，但是他后来为赵国立了两次大功，迅速获得提升。

赵王得到一块极其珍贵的玉璧，秦王很想弄到手，说愿意用十五座城换这块玉璧。赵王知道秦王很狡诈，想找个人去谈这件事，有人推荐了蔺相如。蔺相如接受了任务，来到秦国。秦王看见玉璧就舍不得放手，蔺相如看出秦王没有诚意，就假装说："玉璧上有一点小毛病，请让我指给大王看。"他拿回玉璧，说："如果想抢走它，我的头就与它一起撞碎在柱子上！"秦王请求他不要这样做，他就提出，要秦王布置一个隆重的仪式来接受玉璧。

回到住处后，蔺相如让随从拿着那块玉璧从小路逃走，先把它送回了赵国。等五天后秦王准备接受时，他建议秦国先割让十五座城，然后赵国马上献上玉璧。秦王根本舍不得割让城，又觉得杀了蔺相如也得不到玉璧，反而会破坏秦、赵关系，就客客气气地送他回赵国去了。蔺相如完整地保住了玉璧，又没有激怒秦国，赵王很高兴，马上让他当了高官。

后来，秦军攻打赵国，获得胜利，秦王要求赵王去与他举行和平谈判。赵王本来不敢去，在廉颇、蔺相如等人的劝说下才动身赴会，蔺相如随行。见面之后，秦王喝酒喝得高兴，请赵王弹瑟（sè，中国古代一种弦乐器）；赵王弹完，秦国的史官就写道："某年某月某日，秦王命令赵王弹瑟。"蔺相如也要求秦王敲击一种类似瓦罐的乐器缶（fǒu），秦王不愿意，蔺相如就靠近他说："如果大王不肯敲缶，在五步距离内，我颈子里的血就会溅在您身上!"秦王没有办法，只好敲了一下，蔺相如也马上让赵国史官写道："某年某月某日，秦王为赵王击缶。"此后双方你一言我一语，直到酒宴结束，秦王始终未能占赵国的上风。这次会面结束后回到赵国，赵王就提升蔺相如做了地位最高的官，职位超过廉颇。

廉颇得知这件事后，不服气地说："我做赵国的大将，有许多大功劳，而蔺相如只不过凭着几句言辞立了些功劳，职位却在我之上。再说蔺相如本来地位低微，我不甘心位居他之下!”廉颇扬言若碰见蔺相如，一定要侮辱他。蔺相如听说这件事后，避免跟廉颇见面；出门的时候远远看见廉颇，就掉转车子躲开。

蔺相如的门客觉得这样做太没有面子，说：“廉将军散布一些恶言恶语，您就怕他，躲着他，太过分了。普通人对这种情况尚且感到羞耻，何况是您这种地位的人呢！”门客纷纷要求辞职，蔺相如坚决挽留他们，说：“你们看廉将军与秦王相比谁厉害？”门客回答说：“当然是秦王厉害。”蔺相如说：“我蔺相如敢在秦国的朝廷上斥责秦王，难道会怕廉将军吗？但是强大的秦国之所以不敢轻易侵犯赵国，只因为有我们两个人存在。如果我们争斗起来，受损失的是我们赵国。我这样做，是把国家大事放在前面，而把个人恩怨放在后面。”

有人把这话告诉了廉颇，廉颇非常羞愧。他脱掉上衣，背上绑着荆条，到蔺相如家去请罪，说：“我这个粗鲁无知的人，不知道您宽容我到这样的地步啊！”两人于是和好，成为同生共死的朋友。

# Lian Po and Lin Xiangru

During the Warring States period, the King of Zhao had two competent ministers. One was Lian Po, a grand general, who was brave and resourceful in battle and made great contributions, and the King of Zhao had a very high opinion of him. The other was Lin Xiangru, a civil minister contemporary with Lian Po. Lin was a person of a lower social class at that time, he received rapid promotion because of his tactics.

As the story goes the King of Zhao acquired a priceless jade object and the King of Qin heard about it. The King of Qin coveted the priceless jade and was willing to offer fifteen cities in exchange for it. The King of Zhao knew the King of Qin was a crafty fox and wanted a clever person to handle this matter. Lin was recommended and accepted the task. He went to the State of Qin and saw the King of Qin had no genuine desire to exchange the cities for the priceless jade. The King of Zhao had the jade and he did not wish to have such a priceless artifact slip away. Lin pretended to show the King of Qin a tiny flaw in the jade and then snatched the jade back. Lin then said, "If someone tries to take it back by force, I will break both the jade and his bones!"

The King of Qin asked him not to do that. Lin then made his request that if the King of Qin wanted the jade, a solemn ceremony was absolutely necessary.

After Lin returned to his accommodation, he let his attendant carrying the jade slip secretly away from a path to the State of Zhao. When the King of Qin was ready to accept the jade after five days, Lin suggested the King offer 15 cities in advance and then Zhao would present the priceless jade immediately. The King of Qin didn't want to give the cities away at all. He knew that he also could not get the jade if he killed Lin, which would destroy the relations between Zhao and Qin. So he conveyed Lin back to Zhao decorously. Lin returned the priceless jade intact to the State of Zhao and didn't enrage the King of Qin. The King of Zhao was very happy and let Lin be a senior minister of Zhao at once.

Afterwards, Qin's troops defeated Zhao's and the King of Qin asked the King of Zhao to come to Qin for a peaceful negotiation. The King of Zhao was afraid to go to Qin but went and was accompanied by Lin after being persuaded by Lian Po, Lin Xiangru and other persons. In the banquet, the King of Qin deliberately let the King of Zhao play a Se, a kind of stringed instrument. After the performance, the historiographer of Qin recorded, "that the King of Qin asked the King of Zhao to play a Se at a certain time." Lin requested the King of Qin to play a Fou, a kind of can-shaped drum. The King of Qin was unwilling to play it. Lin came near and threatened him that he was ready to risk his life of the King of Qin didn't play the Fou. The King of Qin had no desire to die and played the Fou. Lin ordered the historiographer of Zhao to write that the King of Qin played the Fou for the King of Zhao at a certain time. The King of Qin was unable to gain the upper hand in the banquet. After they came back to Zhao, Lin was appointed as the Prime Minister of Zhao, which was higher than the post of Lian Po.

However many people were jealous of Lin's success, notably the Grand General Lian Po. Lian thought he was the Grand General of Zhao and had made great contributions to Zhao, while some small fry gained a higher post just by some sweet talking. So Lian didn't submit himself to be Lin's subordinate. He threatened to make trouble for Lin if they met each other. When Lin had caught wind of this, he decided that the best way to deal with the problem was not to confront Lian at all. When Lian's carriage was going down the street, Lin's carriage turned and backed out of the street in order to let Lian Po pass.

Many saw it as a sign of weakness, including Lian Po himself. Lin's courtiers, too, grew dissatisfied by the subservient way Lin was behaving. Many wanted to leave. Lin asked them to stay and said, "Which is more powerful, General Lian or the King of Qin? " The courtiers replied, "Of course the King of Qin." "Who dares rebuke the

King of Qin at the Qin's court, could I be afraid of General Lian? The powerful Qin doesn't invade Zhao easily because of General Lian and I. The feud between me and Lian Po is a personal one, while I cannot let my personal life ruin that of the kingdom!"

When Lian Po finally heard of this, all his hatred turned into shame. Deciding to apologize to Lin, he strapped brambles to his bare back and walked from his house to that of Lin Xiangru's, begging for his forgiveness. Lin forgave him, and from then on, they became good friends.

# 韩信带兵

原文：

hán xìn jiàng bīng，duō duō yì shàn
韩信将兵，多多益善

bá zhì lì zhì，hán xìn zhī jì shèn qí
拔帜立帜，韩信之计甚奇

故事：

推翻秦朝的统治之后，刘邦和项羽为了争做皇帝，又打了将近四年的战争。刘邦最终打败强大的项羽武装，取得胜利，这与他重用具有杰出军事才能的将领韩信有关。在最后的决战中，刘邦一方的军队正是在韩信的指挥下，将楚军彻底击败，从而迫使项羽自杀。

韩信这样一位杰出的人物，年轻时却因为找不到工作，经常依靠别人的帮助才可以勉强吃上饭。很多人都认为他是个没有用的人。后来韩信加入了项羽的军队，项羽对他不重视，给他的职位也不高；他多次给项羽提建议，项羽都没有采纳。韩信知道在项羽这儿没有什么机会了，只好去投奔刘邦的军队。但刘邦也不觉得他有什么特别的地方，只让他做一个管理仓库的小官。他不适合这个工作，还差点因为工作上的失误被处死。

最了解韩信的人，是刘邦最重要的助手、丞相萧何。萧何与韩信交谈过几次，发现了他的军事才华。萧何正打算向刘邦推荐韩信时，韩信却忍受不了这种默默无闻的状况，离开了刘邦的军队。萧何来不及向刘邦报告，便连夜去追赶。有人向刘邦报告说萧何逃跑了，刘邦很震惊。过了一两天，萧何回来，向刘邦说："像韩信这样的人才，天下再没有第二个。您要是只想在这个地方当王，那么不必用他；但若是要争夺天下，只有韩信能帮你实现这个理想。"刘邦还有些迟疑，萧何对他说，要想留住韩信，就得赶紧选个合适的日子，举行隆重的仪式，在众人面前任命韩信为大将，这样才可以。

刘邦同意了萧何的要求。众人听说新的统帅竟是韩信，都觉得很惊讶。刘邦迫不及待地问韩信如何争夺天下这个重大问题。韩信胸有成竹，一条一条地谈他所了解的项羽、刘邦两人各自的优点和缺点，一针见血地指出，项羽虽然名义上是天下的领袖，实际上已失去民心；他建议刘邦将土地分封给立了功的将领，这样他们就会听刘邦的号令，形势很快就会发生变化。刘邦听了，非常欣喜，后悔没有早一点任命韩信为大将，从此在军事上完全听从他的意见。事实证明，

韩信的判断是正确的。

获得汉军的指挥大权后，韩信如鱼得水，充分发挥自己的军事才华，指挥汉军打了很多次精彩的战役。他善于运用多变的战术，灵活用兵，取得了一系列胜利，一点一点地削弱了项羽的力量。项羽这时才发现韩信是一个可怕的对手，派人去劝说韩信背叛刘邦，与他联合，这样就可以三分天下。但韩信认为刘邦对他很好，给了他发挥才能的机会，所以他才有今天的成就，他不愿背叛刘邦。最终，项羽成为韩信的手下败将，走上了绝路。

但刘邦后来也很担心韩信的才能，当上皇帝后，干脆剥夺了韩信对军队的指挥权。韩信闷闷不乐，只好去整理古代的军事著作。

有一次，刘邦与韩信闲谈，讨论将领们才能的高低。刘邦问："我可以指挥多少军队？"韩信说："您可以指挥十万人的军队。"刘邦问："那你呢？"韩信说："我指挥的军队当然是越多越好。"刘邦笑着说："既然如此，你为什么还是被我捉拿了呢？"韩信回答说："您不擅长指挥士兵，但您擅长统率将领，所以我就被您捉住了。您这种能力是天生的，不是努力追求就可以达到的。"可以看出，韩信对自己的带兵作战能力是非常自信的。

# Han Xin in Command of Troops

After the overthrow of the reign of Qin, the war for the throne between Liu Bang and Xiang Yu lasted for four years. Liu finally won the victory which had much to do with Liu's decision of putting Han Xin, a military genius, in an important position. During the final decisive battle, Liu's troops under command of Han Xin defeated Xiang's troops, which forced Xiang to commit suicide.

Han Xin, such a outstanding figure, lived on other's aid because he had been an unemployed youth. Many thought Han was a good-for-nothing fellow. Later, Han Xin joined in Xiang's troops; however, Xiang took little account of him. He had given Xiang suggestions several times, but Xiang thought little of them. Han knew that there was no opportunity to display his talent, so he defected to Liu's troops. However, Liu also didn't think too highly of him and appointed him as a warehouseman. Han was unfit for the job and was nearly executed for mistakes on the job.

Xiao He, Liu's Prime Minister, knew Han Xin well. He found out Han was a military genius after talking with him several times. When Xiao He was about to recommend Han Xin to Liu, Han left Liu's troops, impatient of being a nobody. Xiao He had no time to report to

Liu and instead ran after Han throughout the night. Liu was surprised at the news that Xiao He had run off. Two days later, Xiao He came back and said to Liu, "There is no other talent like Han Xin. If you majesty wants to be King of this place, Han is not essential; if you majesty wants the world, only Han could help you make it come true." When Liu hesitated, Xiao He told him the way to retain Han Xin was to hold a solemn ceremony and appoint him as the Grand General in public.

Liu accepted Xiao He's request. Many were shocked as they found out Han Xin was the new commander-in-chief. Liu could hardly wait to ask Han how to gain his throne. Han already had a thought-out plan and talked with ease and confidence about the merits and demerits of Liu and Xiang. He pointed out that although Xiang had lost the support of people in fact although he still was the nominal ruler of China. Han suggested Liu grant territories to the generals with great achievements to gain their support. Liu was very happy to hear that and regretted that he hadn't trusted Han earlier. From then on, Liu accepted Han's suggestion in military affairs. Facts had proved that Han's judgments were right.

After being the commander-in-chief of Liu's troops, Han brought his military genius into full play and won the battles. He was good at various tactics and weakened Xiang's power step by step. At that time, Xiang found that Han was a terrifying figure and sent people to persuade Han to make an alliance with him against Liu. However, Han was unwilling to betray Liu because Liu gave him the chance to display his talents, which helped him make today's achievements. Finally, Xiang lost to Liu and committed suicide.

Liu was also worried about Han's talents and deprived Han of his

position of general in the military after becoming the emperor of the Han Dynasty. Han was in low spirits and did nothing other than sort out the ancient military works.

Once Liu talked with Han about the talents of generals. Liu asked, "How many troops could I command?" Han replied, "One hundred thousand." "And what about you?" Liu asked. "Of course, the more the better." Han answered. Liu smiled and said, "Since it is so, why are you under my command?" Han answered, "Your Majesty is poor at commanding soldiers but good at commanding generals. That is why I am under your command. Your ability is inborn and cannot be gained by efforts." It shows that Han was very confident in his talents in military affairs.

# 项羽无颜见江东父老

原文：

chǔ xiàng yǔ jiāng dōng yǒu bā qiān zǐ dì
楚项羽江东有八千子弟
wú miàn jiàn jiāng dōng xiàng yǔ xiū guī gù lǐ
无面见江东，项羽羞归故里

故事：

秦朝灭亡之后，项羽与刘邦为了争做皇帝而打了将近四年的战争。项羽勇猛善战，他率领的楚军兵力强大，起初占有优势。但作为一个领袖，他有很多缺点，骄傲自大，对人才不尊重，只知道凭借武力，渐渐失去了民众的支持。刘邦则善于吸引人才，听取不同的意见，最终在垓下（在现在的安徽省灵璧县）包围了缺少粮食的项羽军队。项羽的军队军心涣散，他只得率领少数骑兵突围。著名的京剧《霸王别姬》所讲的故事，就发生在这个时候。

刘邦的汉军紧追不舍。项羽渡过淮河之后，跟随他的骑兵只剩一百多人；后来被汉军围到一座山上，只剩下二十多

人。项羽凭借他的勇力杀死许多汉军，逃到了乌江（在现在的安徽省和县），这时候他的身边剩下的人更少了。乌江这个地方的地方官员仍然保持对项羽的忠诚，他划着船迎接项羽，说："过了江，您就可以回到江东地区了。江东虽然不能说大，但方圆也有千里，人民也有几十万，足以使您继续做国王。希望您赶快渡江，因为这个地方只有我有船，汉军追来的话，也无法渡江追上您。”

江东指的是中国长江下游南岸地区，包括现在的江苏、浙江等省的一部分。长江在安徽境内由西南向东北方向斜流，中国古代以这一段长江为标准，就把上述地区称为江东。项羽从小跟着叔叔一起来到现在的江苏省苏州市，江东是他从小生活的地方。后来项羽和他的叔叔起兵反秦，所依靠的军队，就是来自江东地区的八千人。当初他率领这八千勇敢善战的士兵，来到长江以北地区，仅仅三年时间就消灭了强大的秦朝。但经过与刘邦的连年战争，当初的八千江东士兵都已经被消灭了。

项羽听到乌江地方官员的话，感到很惭愧，他说：“当年我带领八千江东的年轻人渡江，现在他们没有一个人生还。纵然他们的亲人仍然愿意支持我，我哪里还有脸再去见他们呢！”于是他拒绝了这位官员要送他过江的好意，并将自己的马送给这位官员。然后，他回头冲向追来的汉军，杀死了几百人，自己也受了重伤，再也无法战斗了。

项羽看到汉军中有一个将领，这个人以前曾经是他的部下，后来投靠了刘邦，就对这个人说说：“听说汉王刘邦悬赏很多钱、很大的官要我的头，我就为你做件好事吧！”于是他就自刎而死，这一年他只有三十岁。这位曾经不可一世的西楚霸王，就这样结束了他辉煌而悲剧性的一生。

# Xiang Yu Ashamed to Return after a Complete Failure

After the downfall of the Qin Dynasty, the war for the throne between Liu Ban and Xiang Yu lasted for four years. In the beginning, Xiang held an advantage as he was brave and skillful in battle and commanded the powerful troops of Western Chu. However, as a leader, Xiang had many weaknesses such as arrogance, lack of respect for others, advocating military might, and losing the people's support. Liu was good at attracting talents and listening to the advice of others. Finally, Liu's troops encircled Xiang's troops at Gaixia (today's Lingbi County in Anhui Province). Lack of food shook the morale of his troops. Xiang had no choice but to lead a minority of cavalry and escaped the encircling Han troops. The Beijing Opera "Farewell My Concubine" was set at this point in time.

After crossing the Huaihe River, Xiang had only a little more than one hundred soldiers accompanying him. The troops of Han were hot on their heels and later encircled them on a hill. Only twenty soldiers had survived at that point. Xiang killed many Han soldiers and, with a handful of his personal cavalry, finally managed to break out of the morass and headed for Wujiang (today's He County in Anhui Province), where Xiang still enjoyed public support there. A Local official at the river encouraged him to cross the river, telling him that the people of the Jiangdong area were still intent on supporting him as their King. He was the only person who had a boat there, so the troops of Han couldn't catch up with him.

Jiangdong refers to the areas of the southern bank of the lower reaches of the Yangtze River, including today's Jiangsu Province and parts of Zhejiang Province. The Yangtze River within Anhui Province flows from southwest to northeast and was taken as a division in ancient China. Said area was called Jiangdong. Xiang with his uncle lived at Suzhou in Jiangsu Province. So Jiangdong was his hometown. Then, depending on 8,000 soldiers from Jiangdong, Xiang with his uncle raised troops and revolted against the Qin Dynasty. Xiang, with the 8,000 soldiers, destroyed the Qin Dynasty in three years. However, the original 8,000 soldiers nearly died out during the war for the throne between Liu and Xiang.

Words of the local official made Xiang feel ashamed. He said, "I led 8,000 young men across the river that year and they all died. Though their families still support me, I am ashamed to go back." Xiang refused to go across the river and asked the official at the river to send his beloved war horse back to the land of Chu. Then, he headed to the troops of Han, killed hundreds and himself was also seriously

wounded.

When surrounded by the cavalry of Han, Xiang saw a man who once served under him and then went over to Liu and said "I heard Liu offered a great reward for my head. Here let me give you this!" After saying these words, he killed himself and died at the age of 30 years old. The conqueror from Western Chu ended his glorious and tragic life.

Tales of Virtue

美德故事

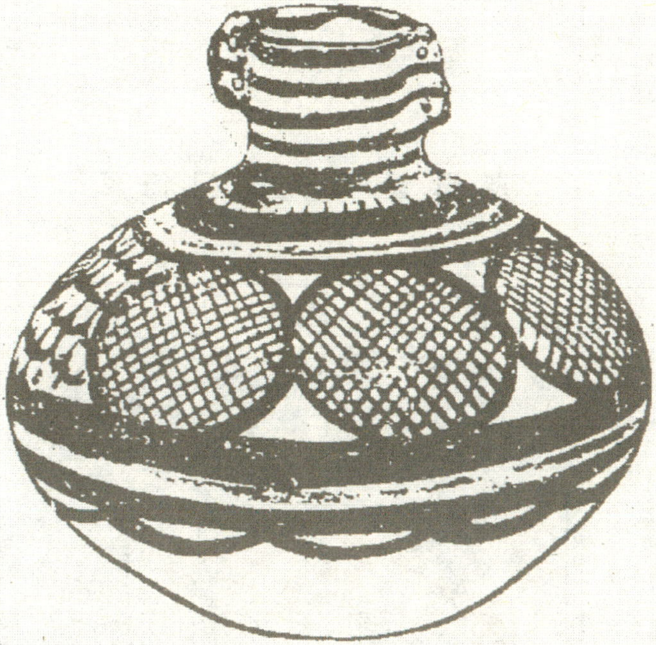

# 王孙贾之母教子

原文：

cí mǔ wàng zǐ, yǐ mén yǐ lǘ
慈母望子，倚门倚闾

故事：

战国时候，齐国有个叫王孙贾的人，十五岁时就在齐国国君齐闵（mǐn）王手下担任官职。他对工作认真负责，经常早出晚归。他的母亲对他很疼爱和关心，每天都在门口等着他回来，如果他回来晚一些，母亲就会很焦急，担心他遇到了什么事。

不久之后，齐国果然发生了很大的变故。齐闵王本来是一个很有作为的君主，在他的治理下，齐国变得很强大，连秦国也畏惧他。他对外发动了很多次战争，都取得了胜利，提高了齐国的威望。但他后来变得骄傲自满，试图夺取更多的土地，这就引起了其他各国的不满。

齐闵王的军队曾经趁着燕（yān）国发生内乱时，攻打并占领了燕国的都城。燕王决心复仇，这时就任命名将乐毅（yuè yì）为统帅，联合了另外四个国家的军队，向齐国发起进攻。齐国孤立无援，连国都也被联军占领了，只剩下三座城没有被攻破，齐闵王逃到其中一座。齐闵王向楚国求救，楚王派将军淖（zhuō）齿率军来见齐闵王，名义上是来帮助齐王，实际上是为了夺取齐国的土地和政权。齐闵王任命淖齿为最高行政长官，没想到淖齿却杀了他，想与燕国一起瓜分齐国的土地。

齐闵王逃跑时，王孙贾等人与他失去了联系，不知他逃到了哪里。大家都不知道该怎么办，年轻的王孙贾也很沮丧，只好回家去。他的母亲在门口等着他，见他回来，却没有像往常一样让他进去，而是拦住门说："以前，你为国家的事情早出晚归，我就靠着家门盼望你回来；等到晚上你还没有回来，我就走到外面的街门那儿去盼望你回来。可是你的职责是为齐王工作，现在他出走了，你竟然不知道他的下落，你为什么不去找齐王，还要回家来呢？"

受到母亲激励的少年王孙贾于是离开家，出去打听齐闵王的下落。当他知道齐闵王的不幸消息时，就走到市场上人群聚集的地方，对人们说："楚国的淖齿在我们齐国作乱，杀害了闵王。谁愿意跟我一起去讨伐淖齿，就露出你们的右臂！"当场就有四百多人跟着王孙贾走了，他们最终找到了淖齿，并将他杀死。齐国军民团结起来抵抗各国军队的入侵，不久之后，收复了大部分国土。

# Wang Sunjia's Mother Educating Her Son

During the Warring States period in the State of Qi, there was a person named Wang Sunjia, who became an official who served the King of Qi when he was fifteen years old. Wang worked hard and left home early and returned late. His mother had much affection and concern for her son. The mother waited for her son to come back home at the door everyday. If he came back a little late, his mother would be very worried about his safety.

Soon after, an unforeseen event occurred in the State of Qin. King Min of Qi was originally a successful ruler. The State of Qi under him became powerful, and even the State of Qin also feared of it. He waged war several times and finally was victorious. The prestige of Qi was improved, while King Min of Qi became arrogant and tried to take more lands, which caused widespread discontent from other states.

His troops had invaded and occupied the Capital of the State of Yan when Yan experienced internal disorder. The King of Yan was determined to take revenge on Qi and appointed Yue Yi, a famous general, as the commander together with troops from four other states to attack Qi. Qi was isolated and cut off from help. Even the Capital of

Qi was taken by the allied troops with only three cities left. King Min of Qi ran away to one of the cities and appealed for help for the State of Chu. The King of Chu sent General Zhuo Chi with troops to meet him. Zhuo Chi gave help to the King of Qi in name, while he in fact came to take the lands and rule Qi himself. King Min of Qi appointed Zhuo Chi as the Supreme Magistrate and did not expect it when the Supreme Magistrate killed him and carved up the lands of Qi with Yan.

When King Min of Qi had run away for the support of other nations, he lost contact with his own people of Qi. No one knew where he was or what to do. Young Wang was very depressed and had no choice but to go home. Waiting at the door, his mother didn't welcome him home as usual when she saw him. She stopped him and said, "I waited for you to come back home before because I knew you were busy with the affairs of state and serving the King of Qi. However, the King is missing now, why don't you go to look for him?"

Encouraged by his mother, young Wan left home and looked for King Min of Qi. When he heard of the bad news about the King, he came to the square where crowds congregated and said, "The state of Qi is stirred up by Zhuo Chi of Chu who killed King Min of Qi. Whoever is willing to kill Zhuo Chi, raise your right arm!" More than 400 people went with Wang and finally killed Zhuo Chi. The troops and

people of Qi united to defend themselves from aggression from other states. Soon afterwards, most lands of Qi were recovered.

# 管宁割席

原文：

guǎn níng gē xí jù huà xīn, wèi fēi tóng zhì zhī rén
管宁割席拒华歆，谓非同志之人

故事：

东汉末年的管宁，从小就性格安静，不向往荣华富贵的生活。他家里很穷，十几岁时父亲就去世了，亲戚朋友们怜悯和同情他，赠送了一些财物让他给父亲办葬礼，可是管宁谢绝了这些财物，以自己真实的财力安葬了父亲。

管宁喜欢研究学术，他结交的朋友也都有同样的兴趣爱好，其中有一个叫华歆（huà xīn）。他们每天一起学习，一起劳动。有一天，管宁和华歆两个人一起在菜园里锄地。管宁的工具碰到一块硬硬的东西，原来是一块不知什么人以前埋藏在地里的黄金，但是管宁把它当作瓦片、石块一样对待，扔到一边，继续挥动工具干活儿。过了一会儿，华歆也看见了这块黄金，将它捡起来看了看，又扔掉了，这情景被管宁看在眼里。

又有一次，两人一起坐在席子上读书。那个时候中国人还没有开始使用椅子这一类的坐具，通常就在地上铺一张席子，坐在它的上面。这时，外面的街上突然传来热闹的人声，原来是一位达官贵人乘坐着华丽的马车经过。管宁好像根本没有听见这种喧闹之声一样，继续认真读书。华歆却坐

不住，把书放下，想跑到门外去看一看。这情景又被管宁看在眼里。管宁认为华歆爱慕荣华富贵，想去当官，就拿了一把刀子，将两人同坐的那张席子从中间割开，说："你不是真正跟我志趣相投的朋友！"

两位好朋友就这样分开了，各自走上了自己选择的道路。后来因为天下大乱，管宁跑到局势比较安定的辽东去避难，辽东就是现在的辽宁省和吉林省一带。当地的官员对他很尊重，但他不愿接受官职和财物，住在自己建的简陋房子里。他在辽东生活了三十七年。曹操死后，他的儿子曹丕（pī）建立了魏国，请管宁回去当官。管宁回到中原，却坚决推辞了魏国皇帝的任命。

这个时候，华歆已经在魏国做到了很高的官职，他做官的声誉很好，推行了一些对人民有利的政策。虽然经过了"割席绝交"这样的事件，华歆仍然把管宁看作朋友，他欣赏管宁的才学和品德，屡次推荐管宁担任重要官职，甚至愿意将自己的职位让给管宁。魏国皇帝以很高的规格去邀请管宁，但管宁仍然不愿意做官，而是按照自己年轻时的志愿，继续从事研究和写作。

# Guan Ning Cuts the Mat

"Guan Ning Cuts the Mat" is a Chinese idiom that comes from a story in the Three Kingdoms Period. During the late Eastern Han Dynasty, there was a diligent learner named Guan Ning, who was quiet and indifferent to fame and wealth. He was born in a poor family. When his father died, he was only in his teens. Friends and relatives had sympathy for him and gave him some properties for his father's funeral, but Guan politely refused such help and buried his father by his own efforts.

Guan liked academic research, and so did his friends. At that time, he and Hua Xin were very good school friends. They studied and did farm work together everyday. One day while they were hoe-

ing in their garden, Guan dug out a bar of gold. Guan went on hoeing without giving the find a second glance, while Hua Xin picked it up, regarded it for a moment then threw it away.

Another day the two friends were reading together on the same mat (at that time the Chinese hadn't started to use chairs or stools) when there arose great shouting outside the study window as a high-ranking official was passing by in his luxuriously decorated carriage. Guan continued to read but Hua Xin dropped his book and wanted to go out for a better view. Guan thought Hua Xin admired high social status and power and felt more and more disgusted with Hua Xin. So he drew out a dagger and cut the mat they were sitting on in two, separating himself from Hua Xin, and said, "You are not my real friend!"

Soon the two parted and each went their separate ways. China was in confusion later. Guan fled to Liaodong (today's Liaoning and Jilin provinces) to live the life of a hermit. The local officials respected him very much but he was unwilling to accept the position of an official or the properties they offered him. He lived in his barely furnished house in Liaodong for 37 years. After the death of Cao Cao, his son Cao Pi established the State of Wei and invited Guan back to be an official. Guan came back to Wei but declined the invitation of Cao Pi.

Hua Xin became a high-ranking official of Wei and enjoyed great fame. He carried out beneficial policies for the civilans and still regarded Guan to be his friend in spite of the events of "Guan Ning Cuts the Mat". In appreciation of Guan's learning and moral character, Hua Xin had recommended Guan for an important position many times and even gave him his own position. Cao Pi had invited Guan with full ceremony but he was still unwilling to be an official and went on with academic research and writing of his own will.

# 陶渊明不为五斗米折腰

原文：

bú wèi mǐ zhé yāo, táo yuān míng bú bài lì xū
不为米折腰，陶渊明不拜吏胥

故事：

陶渊明生活在东晋（317—420）末年，祖先是东晋的开国元勋陶侃（kǎn），祖父和父亲也做过地方长官。陶渊明九岁时父亲就去世了，他与母亲和妹妹去投奔外祖父。外祖父生活不富裕，但喜欢喝酒和读书，性格自然洒脱，陶渊明深受他的影响。

陶家家境贫寒，没有多少田地，经常缺少粮食。等陶渊明长大了，亲戚朋友们都劝他出去当官，以养活家庭。陶渊明于是就去找工作，先后担任过一些低级官职。在当官的过程中，他接触到了更多的社会现实。陶渊明本来也想在政治上有所作为，但他的职位很低，根本无法实现自己的理想，还不得不做很多违心的事。当时东晋王朝的统治很黑暗、腐

败，整个社会动荡不安。他看清了这种社会现实后，感到厌恶和绝望，于是萌发了回到家乡隐居的念头。

他最后担任的官职是彭泽县（在现在的江西省）的地方官，这个职位是他的叔叔帮他谋求来的。但在这个职位上，他必须处理很多繁琐的行政事务，还经常要应酬上级官员，这与他洁身自好、崇尚自然的本性格格不入，他为此很苦恼。

不久之后，上级派了一个巡察官到彭泽县来考察他的工作。这位巡察官粗俗而傲慢，刚到县里，就派人来下达命令，要求陶渊明马上去拜见他。陶渊明穿着日常的衣服，正准备动身，他手下的职员拦住他，吃惊地说："按照规矩，您应该穿上整整齐齐的官服，才能去见巡察官，否则他就会不高兴，在上级面前说您的坏话。"

陶渊明无法再忍受不下去，长叹一声说："我不能为了拿到五斗（dǒu）米，就恭恭敬敬向这种庸俗小人弯腰行礼！"斗是中国古代计量粮食的容量单位，五斗米的意思是说地方官的收入不高。陶渊明说完之后，写了一封辞职信，就离开了彭泽县。他在这个县只做了八十多天的地方官。

陶渊明回到家乡的乡村，开始自己耕种田地养活全家。虽然生活很贫困，但他始终没有再去做官。在隐居生活中，他惊喜地发现了大自然和乡村生活的美好，并通过诗歌和散文表达出他的感受。他的作品语言质朴自然，达到了极高的艺术水平，表现出热爱自然、超越世俗的志趣。他喜欢酒和菊花，这两样东西经常出现在他的作品里。

后来的文学家和普通读者都很推崇陶渊明的高尚人格和文学成就，认为他是真正的田园诗人。

# Won't Kowtow for Five Dous of Rice

Tao Yuanming was a renowned hermit and outstanding poet in the Eastern Jin Period(317–420). His great-grandfather, Tao Kan, was a founding father of Eastern Jin, and his grandfather and father had also been magistrates. When he was nine years old, his father died. So his mother took all four of her children, Tao Yuanming and his three sisters, to her father for shelter. Though the family was also not well off, his maternal grandfather was extraordinarily free and easy in character and fond of drinking and reading, which greatly influenced Tao Yuanming.

The Tao family was very poor with little farmland and lacking of food and clothes. When he grew up, he followed the idea of friends and relatives to serve as an official. He dealt with social reality and had hoped to do something in politics, but he was not that important and was looked down upon in the imperial court's stern hierarchical system. He wearied of the dark life of an official and despaired of the social reality, before coming up with the idea of returning home to live in seclusion.

His last official position was as the magistrate of Pengze County (in today's Jiangxi Province) under the help of his uncle. At that time, he had to handle lots of trivial civil affairs and engaged in social activities with superior officials. He didn't fit in with such a life and felt distressed.

Soon afterwards, a senior official came to inspect the county. The senior official was not only vulgar but also arrogant and ordered Tao to meet him at once. Tao 's aide urged him to make haste and change his casual wear into his best regalia, or the senior official would be angry and speak evil of him.

Tao couldn't stick it out any longer and there upon retorted, "I will not dress myself up and kowtow to this pretentious bumpkin just for five dous of rice", referring to his salary as an official, as a dou was the measuring unit of foodstuffs in ancient China. After saying that, he handed in his official seal and returned home from the county where he served as an official for 80 days.

After he returned home, Tao led a self-supporting farming life in the countryside. Although he was poor and had to work hard, he was satisfied with the tranquil life and never thought of political life again. As a hermit, he enjoyed the beauty of nature and life and expressed his feelings by poems and prose. His works, with simple and unpretentious language, had reached a high artistic level and showed his love of nature and his refined interests. He was fond of both drinking and

chrysanthemums, which were often found in his works.

Scholars and readers in later times praised highly his unbending lofty sentiments and his achievements in literature and regarded him as a real "pastoral poet".

# Tales of Talents
# 人才故事

# 西门豹破除陋习

原文：

xī mén bào xìng jí，cháng pèi wéi yǐ zì kuān
西门豹性急，常佩韦以自宽

故事：

战国时候，魏国有个人叫西门豹，被魏王派到邺县（在现在的河北省临漳县）去做地方长官。西门豹到了邺县，看到当地很荒凉、萧条，就找了一些老人，问他们有什么痛苦的事。这些人说："因为每年要给河神娶新娘，本地人民都变得很贫困。"

西门豹问这是怎么回事，人们向他解释，当地有一条河，经常发洪水，危害人们的生活。巫师们认为这是风流的河神想要娶新娘，假如不把新娘送给河神，就会大水泛滥，把大家都淹死，所以当地每年都要举行为河神娶新娘的活动。地方官员们趁机向人们征收钱财，收取几百万钱，他们只用其中的二三十万为河神娶新娘，剩下的就由官员和巫师们拿回自己家了。女巫看到哪一家有漂亮的女儿，就说："这个女孩适合做河神的新娘。"于是给这女孩穿上漂亮衣服，又把一张席子装饰好，让女孩坐在上面。巫师把席子放到河水里，席子起初在水面上漂浮着，漂到河中间便沉没了。有漂亮女儿的人家大多带着女儿逃到远方，因此当地人口越来越少。

西门豹听了这话，非常愤怒。他本来是个很性急的人，为了告诫自己不要冲动，就随身佩戴一块经过加工的柔软牛皮。他摸着这块牛皮，压制着怒火说："到了给河神娶新娘的那天，我也要到河边去观看。"当地官员和巫师们听到这个消息，认为西门豹跟以前的长官一样纵容和支持他们，都很高兴。

到了那一天，西门豹来到河边，地方官员、巫师和有钱有势的人都聚集在这里，在旁边观看的民众也有两三千人。女巫的首领是个七十岁的老巫婆，她手下还有十几个女巫。西门豹说："把新娘子带过来，我看看她长得漂亮不漂亮。"这个可怜的女孩来到西门豹面前，西门豹看了看，说："这个女孩不漂亮，麻烦大巫婆到河里去禀报河神，我需要重新找一个美女，过几天再送去。"就叫部下抱起大巫婆，把她扔到河里。过了一会儿，西门豹说："巫婆为什么去这么久还不回来？让她的徒弟去看看！"又把一个女巫扔进河里。再过了一会儿，西门豹说："这个徒弟为什么也很久不回来？再派一个人去催催她们！"又扔了一个女巫到河中。

扔了三个年轻女巫后，西门豹说："大巫婆和她的徒弟都是女人，不能把事情说清楚，还是请地方官替我去说明情况吧。"又把一个地方官员扔到河中。等了很久，当然，这个官员也没有回来，其他官员都很惊慌。西门豹说："巫婆和那位地方官都不回来，怎么办呢？”他下令再派一个人去，结果其他官员都吓得在地上磕头求饶，把头都磕破了，血流了一地，脸色非常难看。西门豹说：“看样子河神要把这些客人长时间留在他那儿，你们还是离开这儿回家去吧。”那些借口给河神娶新娘从而获得钱财的人都非常惊恐，不敢再提这件事。而邺县的人民知道从此不用再为这个骗局而痛苦，都高高兴兴地回家去了。

后来，西门豹带着老百姓挖了十二条渠道，把河水引来灌溉农田。这样，洪水不再发作，而田地则获得了好收成。当地人民的生活变得富裕，逃到外地的人也逐渐回来，邺县变成了一个繁华的地方。

# Ximen Bao Did away with Feudal Custom

During the Warring States period, there was a talented person named Ximen Bao, who was appointed as the magistrate of Ye County (today's Linzhang County in Hebei Province) by the King of Wei. When he took up residency in the county, he was surprised by the low population density and depressed economy there. He summoned a meeting with the elders of the district and asked them whether they had any trouble.

They replied that because the river god wanted to get married every year, local people became miserably poor.

Ximen Bao asked the reason and was told that there was a river, which often flooded and became a serious danger to the normal life of local people. And witches told them that it was because the river god wanted a beautiful bride every year. If people refused the demand of the river god, he would cause the river to swell and inundate their farmlands and houses. Every year the local officials asked them to donate money of several millions but they only spent about twenty per cent of this amount on the celebration of the river god's wedding and the rest of the money was divided amongst themselves. If the witches saw a beautiful girl they would say, "This is a beautiful girl who would be the next wife for the river god". Then the poor girl would be dressed up and arranged to sit on a decorated mat. The witches would put the mat with the girl into the river. After drifting for a while, the mat would sink and the poor girl drowned. People were frightened that their daughters would be chosen as the brides for the river god. So, many families moved away from this district. That is why there are not many people living there.

Ximen Bao was a quick-tempered person and felt angry to hear that. In order to warn himself not to be impetuous, he stroked a piece of refined soft cowhide taken with him to restrain his anger and asked to be informed when the next wedding was due. The local officials and witches were very happy after hearing this news and thought Ximen Bao would support them as had other officials.

The day of the next wedding arrived and as usual the local witch, the local gentry, the local officials and all the citizens numbering a few thousand who came from far and near. The local witch, a 70-year-old woman, came with tens of disciples. Ximen Bao demanded to see the bride before she was given away to the river god. His conclusion was that the girl was not beautiful enough and a new girl should be found, so the witch should inform the river god. He asked some of his soldiers to accompany the local witch to the river bed. Without any delay the soldiers threw the witch into the river. After waiting for some time Ximen Bao complained that the local witch was taking too long and should have been back already. He ordered one of her disciples to go and see what had happened to her mistress. Down she went to the river

and a few soldiers grabbed her and tossed her into the river. Again nothing happened in the river. Ximen Bao was a bit annoyed. He ordered another disciple to go down to the river bed and report back to him without delay. This disciple was similarly hurled into the river.

Unhappy that the local witch and her disciples had not yet returned, he told one of the local officials to go and find out what had happened. The soldiers took this official and dumped him into the river. After a long wait, the witches and the local official had not yet returned. He wanted another local official to investigate. Immediately, the local officials kneeled down and kowtowed to Ximen Bao to beg for mercy and forgiveness. Then Ximen Bao said, "It seems that the river god would like them stay longer, so you could leave and go home." The people who had devised such a dirty trick were frightened and no one dared to bring up the matter again. The People of Ye County were very happy that they needn't suffer the dirty trick by these swindlers.

Afterwards, Ximen Bao led the local people and dug 12 trenches to divert water from the river to irrigate their farmlands. The river didn't flood, while the farmlands had good harvests. More and more ex-residents gradually returned to live in the district. Ye County became prosperous.

# 陶侃物尽其用

原文：

mù xiè zhú tóu, jiē wéi yǒu yòng zhī wù
**木屑竹头，皆为有用之物**

故事：

陶侃就是前面讲到的东晋大诗人陶渊明的曾祖父。他是一位杰出的将军，为东晋立下很多功劳。他也是一位很有成就的地方行政长官，既聪明又勤奋，受到人们的称赞。他的远见卓识和管理才能不仅体现在解决重大事件方面，也经常表现在一些细小的方面。

陶侃曾经在广州（在现在的广东省）担任行政长官。他在书房里准备了一百块砖，没事的时候，总是早晨把这些砖全部搬到外面，晚上又把它们再搬回书房。别人不明白他为什么要这样做，他回答说："我将来要努力收复被敌人占领的中原地区，如果现在生活太舒服、太轻松，恐怕以后不能承担大事，所以才这样锻炼身体。"

后来他又被派去担任荆州（在现在的湖北省）的地方长官，工作非常认真负责。当时政府正在造船，他要求负责建造船只的官员把锯木头剩下的木屑全都收集起来，保存在适当的地方，大家都不明白他为什么要这么做。转眼就到了中国农历的正（zhēng）月初一，按照惯例，地方长官要在这天会见手下所有的官员。大家都赶到处理政事的大厅，正好前几天一直下雪，刚刚转晴，大厅前的台阶上都是融化的雪水，很不好走。陶侃让人取出那些保存起来的木屑，铺在这些台阶上，于是大家进进出出都很方便。

政府使用竹子，会砍下末端没用的部分，陶侃叫人把这些竹头收集起来，时间长了，堆积得像一座小山。后来东晋的大将桓温进攻四川，需要把战船连接起来，于是当年陶侃收集起来的这些竹头就都用来做了钉子。在处理其他事情时，陶侃也都会这样全面、细密地考虑。

在陶侃的影响下，他的下属也都养成了使物品充分发挥作用的思维习惯。他曾经让下属准备一些撑船用的竹竿。一般的做法是，将竹子的根部砍掉，然后装上一个铁制的部件。有一个官员把竹子连根拔出来，试着用竹子的根部代替那个铁制部件，发现效果很好，因此节省了铁制部件。陶侃知道这件事后，就把这个官员提升了两级。

# Tao Kan Made the Best Use of Things

Tao Kan, the great grandfather of Tao Yuanming, was an outstanding general and made great contributions to the Eastern Jin Dynasty. He was also a successful magistrate and was praised highly by the people. His foresight and sagacity as well as managerial aptitude not

only showed in important events but also in trivial matters.

When Tao once was appointed as the magistrate of Guangzhou (in today's Guangdong Province). he put one hundred bricks in his study room and carried them out of the room in the morning and took them back into the room in the evening in his spare time. When others asked why he did that, he replied, "I will try my best to regain the lost territory from our enemies in the future. If I live in comfort and ease, I'm afraid I will not be able to undertake these important tasks. So I do exercises like this."

Later, he was appointed as the magistrate of Jingzhou (in today's Hubei Province). He worked hard and seriously. At that time, the local government was busy with shipbuilding, while he ordered the officials responsible for shipbuilding to collect all the waste wood chips left by sawing wood and store them in the proper place. No one knew why he did that. Time went on. On the first day of the first month of the lunar new year, according to usual practice, the magistrate would meet all subordinate officials. Everyone headed to the hall. Because of the snow which had stopped just then, the steps before the hall were very wet and slippery because of the melten snow. Tao ordered people to take out the well-kept wood chips and put them on the steps. So, it was very convenient for the people's coming and going.

The government utilized bamboo and left the useless top and end parts. Tao ordered people to collect them. As time went on, they were piled high as a hill. Later, the Grand General Huan Wen of Eastern Jin needed warships to attack Sichuan. So, the top and end parts of the bamboo collected by Tao were made into bamboo nails. When handling other matters, Tao was also very clever.

Under his influence, his subordinates also formed habits of using the best of the things. Once he ordered the subordinate officials to prepare some bamboo for punting. The common practice was to cut off the end part of the bamboo and install the iron parts. One official pulled up the bamboo by the root and tried to replace the iron parts with the roots. The roots worked well, so iron parts were saved. This official was promoted two ranks after Tao heard of this matter.

# 曹植才高八斗

原文：

zhǔ dòu rán qí，wèi qí xiāng hài
煮豆燃萁，谓其相害
duō cái zhī shì，cái chǔ bā dǒu
多才之士，才储八斗
qí bù qí cái，xiàn tiān cái zhī mǐn jié
七步奇才，羡天才之敏捷
zhǔ dòu rán qí，bǐ xiōng cán dì
煮豆燃萁，比兄残弟

故事：

在中国古代，人们夸赞某个人很有才华，就会说“他的才华像曹子建一样突出”，或者说“他才高八斗”。曹子建就是曹植，他是三国时期（220—280）北方统治者曹操的第三个儿子，是中国历史上有名的文学家。

曹植从小就非常聪明，十几岁时就能背诵几十万字的文章和诗歌,表现出写作方面的天赋。有一次，曹操新建了一座宫殿，让当时有名的文人一起来写文章纪念。曹植第一个完成

了文章，而且写得很精彩，曹操看后了非常高兴。曹植也努力学习骑马、射箭和打仗的本领，曾多次跟随曹操出征，都取得了胜利。曹操对他很宠爱，想让他成为自己的继承人。

但是曹植的哥哥曹丕同样文武双全，同样渴望成为王位的继承人。曹丕暗中与曹植展开争斗。而曹植呢，仗着自己才华出众，有些骄傲，行为不谨慎，多次违反法令。有一次，曹操想派曹植带兵出征，但曹植正好喝醉了，无法前来接受任命。就这样，曹操也逐渐对曹植失望了，认为他更适合当个自由自在的文学家，而不是承担国家大事的政治家。最终，行为稳健、富有智谋的曹丕获得了王位继承权。曹操病死之后，曹丕建立了魏国，成为皇帝。

曹丕做了皇帝，可是仍然对曹植不放心，想方设法限制他的自由。有一次，曹丕找了一些理由，打算惩罚曹植。因为大家都夸赞曹植有突出的才华，曹丕就命令他在走七步的时间内写出一首诗来，规定内容是关于兄弟关系的；如果做不出诗，就要定他的罪。同情曹植的人都为他担心，而曹植却不慌不忙，还没有走完七步路，就念出他所写的诗。这首诗的大意是说，锅里面正在煮着豆子，而锅下面燃烧的则是豆茎；豆子渗出汁水，好像在哭泣，它问豆茎：本来我们是同一条根上生长出来的，你为什么这样急不可待地想煮死我呢？听到这首悲伤而寓意深刻的诗，曹丕觉得很惭愧，就没有杀曹植，只是降低了他的爵位。这首诗后来广泛流传，用来比喻兄弟之间互相残杀的情形。

虽然保全了性命，但曹植仍然处处受限制和打击，过着很不自由、很不快乐的生活。他借助诗歌来表现自己苦闷的心情和渴望为国家建功立业的理想，这些诗歌艺术成就很高，对后世文学家的影响很大。

曹丕死后，他的儿子继承了皇帝之位，对曹植仍然严加防范和限制。曹植心情苦闷，就在这样的处境中去世了。他的文学成就受到后人的景仰。

过了大约两个世纪，南北朝（420—589）的时候，中国出现了一位著名诗人谢灵运，他发表评论说："天下的文学才华一共有一石（dàn），曹子建一个人独自拥有八斗，我拥有一斗，其他人分享剩下的那一斗。"石是中国古代计量粮食的容量单位，一石等于十斗。他这个评论，把曹植推到了很高的地位；当然，他对自己的评价也很高。此后，中国人在称赞一个人很有才华时，常常说他"才高八斗"。

# Cao Zhi of Great Literary Talent

In ancient China, if people wanted to praise somebody with talent, they would say, "Somebody has eight deciliters of talent", which means somebody is of great literary talent or somebody is as outstanding as Cao Zijian in talent. Cao Zijian was Cao Zhi, a famous litterateur in history and also the third son of the powerful warlord Cao Cao in the Three Kingdoms Period (220–280).

Cao Zhi was very clever and could recite more than ten thousand verses worth of poems before he even turned twenty. He also had a great aptitude for writing. Once Cao Cao built a palace and let the famous litterateurs at that time write articles as a memorial. Cao Zhi completed his article first. His article was brilliant, which pleased Cao Cao. He also worked hard at horse riding, archery and other abilities in battle. He had accompanied Cao Cao to go out for battles many times and helped him win. Cao Cao favored him very much and wanted to name Cao Zhi as his successor.

However, Cao Pi, brother of Cao Zhi, was also well versed in both literature and martial arts and aspired to become the successor of Cao Cao. Behind the scenes, Cao Pi and Cao Zhi fought for position.

Cao Zhi was an impetuous man with little self-discipline and great arrogance. He had violated his father's decrees many times. Once, Cao Cao wanted to send Cao Zhi to go out for a battle, but Cao Zhi was drunk and unable to accept the order. So, Cao Cao gradually lost faith in him and thought Cao Zhi was a suitable scholar instead of a politician able to undertake the affairs of state. Finally, the moderate Cao Pi with worldly wisdom became the successor of Cao Cao. After the death of Cao Cao, Cao Pi established the Kingdom of Wei and became the Emperor of Wei.

Though being the emperor, Cao Pi was still afraid Cao Zhi might cause problems, so he always was looking for a way to restrain Cao Zhi. Once, Cao Pi wanted to punish Cao Zhi and found some excuses. Jealous of Cao Zhi's talent, Cao Pi ordered Cao Zhi to walk seven steps and within the duration of time he should compose a poem with content of brotherhood. As he was extraordinarily talented, Cao Zhi had already finished his poem before he finished walking the seven steps. His poem was: "Beanstalks burned to cook beans,/ But in the pot beans weep,/ Grown from the same stems,/ Why boil me in such an attempt?" After hearing the sad and meaningful poem, Cao Pi grew ashamed and gave up his attempts to kill Cao Zhi. This poem later went round and is now used to describe the act of doing harm to one's brother or mutual slaughter between brothers.

Though his life was saved, Cao Zhi was imprisoned and beaten. He expressed his distress and ideal of making contributions to the

kingdom by poems, which had high achievements of art and exerted great influence on the litterateurs of the later generations.

After the death of Cao Pi, the son of Cao Pi took over the throne and kept Cao Zhi imprisoned as well. Cao Zhi lived in mental distress and died under such circumstance. His literary achievements were praised highly by the later generations.

Around two hundred years later, there was a famous poet named Xie Lingyun in the Northern and Southern Dynasties (420–589). He commented on Cao Zhi and said, "If all talent of the world is calculated by ten decalitres, Cao Zhi himself would account for eight deciliters, while I would account for one decalitre, the remaining one decalitre for others." According to his comment, he thought highly of Cao Zhi, and of course himself. Thereafter, the Chinese often use "somebody has eight deciliters of talent" to describe a talent.

# 张僧繇画龙

原文：

zhāng sēng yóu huà bì lóng， diǎn jīng zé léi diàn ér fēi téng
**张僧繇画壁龙，点睛则雷电而飞腾**

故事：

张僧繇(yóu)是南北朝时期梁朝（502—557）的画家，擅长画人物画像、龙、鹰等，很善于表现佛教题材。梁的第一个皇帝梁武帝喜好佛教，建了很多佛教寺庙，而这些寺庙中的壁画，大都是张僧繇画的。

张僧繇练习绘画非常勤奋，无论什么时候，手里都握着画笔；他不分白天黑夜地辛勤作画，几十年间从未松懈。经过这样的勤学苦练，他的绘画技艺达到了极其高超的境界，创造了多种精妙的表现手法。他画的人物、动物神态生动，好像活的一样。许多学画者都把他看成是学习的榜样。

中国古代流传着很多关于张僧繇和他的画的神奇传说。有一个传说是这样的，有座寺庙塑造了威严高大的佛像，但

令人头疼的是，有一些鸟雀停在房梁上面休息，它们拉下的粪便玷（diàn）污了佛像。寺庙里的僧人将张僧繇请去，让他想办法。张僧繇在东面的墙壁上画了一只鹰，在西面的墙壁上画了另外一只凶猛的鸟，这两只鸟都侧着头向檐外睨（nì）视。从此，那些鸟雀再也不敢到佛殿的屋梁上来了。

最神奇的是关于张僧繇画龙的传说。梁的都城金陵（在现在的江苏省南京市）有一座寺院叫安乐寺，张僧繇到那儿去游玩，寺里的僧人听说他就是那位著名的画家，就请求他在寺庙的墙壁上面画他最擅长的龙。张僧繇在墙壁上画了四条龙。画成之后，有人一看，发现这些龙都没有眼睛，以为张僧繇忘记了，就提醒他，张僧繇回答说：“只要画上眼睛，龙就会飞走的。”观看的人都认为他说的话很荒唐，不相信有这种事，坚持请他给龙画上眼睛。张僧繇提起画笔，刚刚给其中两条龙点上眼睛，天上突然电闪雷鸣，雷电击穿墙壁，两条龙驾着云向天空中飞去，很快就不见了踪影。人们惊讶极了，再回头看时，墙上只剩下还没有画上眼睛的两条龙。

据说张僧繇创造了一种新的画人物的方法，画出的人物比较丰满，到了隋（581—618）、唐（618—907）时期，这种画法非常流行。可惜的是，这位优秀画家的作品后来全部失传，现在我们已欣赏不到他神奇的绘画艺术了。

# Zhang Sengyou Drawing Chinese Dragons

In the Liang Dynasty (502–557) there lived a painter called Zhang Sengyou, who excelled at drawing dragons and eagles as well as figures of Buddha. The first emperor of Liang was a Buddhist and built many temples, however, most mural paintings in the temples were drawn by Zhang Sengyou.

As an industrious painter, Zhang held his paintbrush all the time and painted at all hours of the day and night for decades. After diligent study and hard training, his painting techniques had reached a high level and he had created many masterful techniques of expression. The figures under his paintbrush were vivid and looked like real people. Many students of painting regarded him as their role model.

In ancient China there went around many legends about Zhang and his paintings. One goes that a temple built a tall and majestic Buddhist statue, but a troublesome problem was that when some sparrows rested on the beam of the hall, birds droppings always fell on the statue, which greatly profaned the statue. Monks of the temple invited Zhang to the temple to give them some advice. Zhang drew a eagle on the eastern wall and a ferocious curassow on the western wall with cocking heads looking askance at the eaves. Henceforth, those sparrows daren't rest on the ceiling beam.

The most magical story was the one about Zhang Sengyou painting dragons without eyes. There was a temple called Anle Temple at Jinling (today's Nanjing in Jiangsu Province), the Capital of Liang.

One day, Zhang visited the temple. Monks of the temple had heard of him and asked him to draw dragons on the wall of the temple. His mural contained four dragons. The dragons were wonderfully lifelike, however, none of the four dragons had any eyes. Someone reminded him of it. And he replied, "If I had painted eyes, the dragons would have been so realistic they would have flown away." Those who heard this didn't believe it. They asked Zhang to try painting in the dragons' eyes. Zhang lifted his brush and carefully began to paint in the eyes of the dragons. He had just painted in the eyes of the second dragon when suddenly there was a mighty flash of lightning and a great clap of thunder. Everyone scattered in fear. When they came back they saw that the wall had cracked open, and the two dragons whose eyes had been painted in had disappeared. But the two dragons whose eyes had not been painted were still there on the wall.

It is said that Zhang created a new technique of figure drawing, which made the figure well-rounded and was very popular during the Sui (581–618) and Tang (618–907) dynasties. Unfortunately, all works of this famous painter were lost. So, we are unable to appreciate his magical techniques of painting.

# 《幼学琼林》精选

## 卷一

hùn dùn chū kāi qián kūn shǐ diàn
混沌初开，乾坤始奠。

shēn shāng èr xīng qí chū mò bù xiāng jiàn
参商二星，其出没不相见；

niú nǚ liǎng xiù wéi qī xī yì xiāng féng
牛女两宿，惟七夕一相逢。

hòu yì qī bēn yuè gōng ér wéi cháng é
后羿妻，奔月宫而为嫦娥；

fù yuè sǐ qí jīng shén tuō yú jī wěi
傅说死，其精神托于箕尾。

xīn duō guò lǜ hé yì qǐ rén yōu tiān
心多过虑，何异杞人忧天；

shì bú liàng lì, bù shū kuā fù zhuī rì
事不量力，不殊夸父追日。

cāng hǎi sāng tián, wèi shì shì zhī duō biàn
沧海桑田，谓世事之多变；

hé qīng hǎi yàn, zhào tiān xià zhī shēng píng
河清海晏，兆天下之升平。

yǐ lí cè hǎi, yù rén zhī jiàn xiǎo
以蠡测海，喻人之见小；

jīng wèi xián shí, bǐ rén zhī tú láo
精卫衔石，比人之徒劳。

dào bù shí yí, yóu zài shàng yǒu shàn zhèng
道不拾遗，由在上有善政；

hǎi bù yáng bō, zhī zhōng guó yǒu shèng rén
海不扬波，知中国有圣人。

duān yáng jìng dù, diào qū yuán zhī nì shuǐ
端阳竞渡，吊屈原之溺水；

chóng jiǔ dēng gāo, xiào huán jǐng zhī bì zāi
重九登高，效桓景之避灾。

wǔ wù jī tún yàn shè chù chù yǐn zhì lóng zhī jiǔ
五戊鸡豚宴社，处处饮治聋之酒；

qī xī niú nǚ dù hé jiā jiā chuān qǐ qiǎo zhī zhēn
七夕牛女渡河，家家穿乞巧之针。

zhōng qiū yuè lǎng mínghuáng qīn yóu yú yuè diàn
中秋月朗，明皇亲游于月殿；

jiǔ rì fēng gāo mèng jiā mào luò yú lóng shān
九日风高，孟嘉帽落于龙山。

yǐ shù yú rén yuē zhāo sān mù sì
以术愚人，曰朝三暮四；

wéi xué qiú yì yuē rì jiù yuè jiāng
为学求益，曰日就月将。

xiāo cáo xiàng hàn gāo céng wéi dāo bǐ lì
萧曹相汉高，曾为刀笔吏；

jí àn xiàng hàn wǔ zhēn shì shè jì chén
汲黯相汉武，真是社稷臣。

fàn zhòng yān xiōng zhōng jù shù wàn jiǎ bīng
范仲淹胸中具数万甲兵，

chǔ xiàng yǔ jiāngdōng yǒu bā qiān zǐ dì
楚项羽江东有八千子弟。

hán xìn jiàng bīng duō duō yì shàn
韩信将兵，多多益善；

máo suí jī zhòng lù lù wú qí
毛遂讥众，碌碌无奇。

fú jiān zì kuā jiàngguǎng tóu biān kě yǐ duàn liú
苻坚自夸将广，投鞭可以断流；

máo suí zì jiàn cái qí chǔ náng biàn dāng tuō yǐng
毛遂自荐才奇，处囊便当脱颖。

xiū yǔ kuài děng wǔ hán xìn jiàng zuò huái yīn
羞与哙等伍，韩信降作淮阴；

wú miàn jiàn jiāngdōng xiàng yǔ xiū guī gù lǐ
无面见江东，项羽羞归故里。

## 卷二

shēng zǐ dāng rú sūn zhòng móu cáo cāo xiàn sūn quán zhī yǔ
生子当如孙仲谋，曹操羡孙权之语；

shēng zǐ xū rú lǐ yà zǐ, zhū wēn tàn cún xù zhī cí
生子须如李亚子，朱温叹存勖之词。

cí mǔ wàng zǐ, yǐ mén yǐ lǘ
慈母望子，倚门倚闾；

yóu zǐ sī qīn, zhì hù zhì qǐ
游子思亲，陟岵陟屺。

dōngzhēng pò fǔ, zhōugōng dà yì miè qīn
东征破斧，周公大义灭亲；

yù zéi zhēng sǐ, zhào xiào yǐ shēn dài dì
遇贼争死，赵孝以身代弟。

zhǔ dòu rán qí, wèi qí xiāng hài
煮豆燃萁，谓其相害；

dǒu sù chǐ bù, jī qí bù róng
斗粟尺布，讥其不容。

bú qì zāo kāng, sònghóng huí guāng wǔ zhī yǔ
不弃糟糠，宋弘回光武之语；

jǔ àn qí méi, liánghóng pèi mèngguāng zhī xián
举案齐眉，梁鸿配孟光之贤。

wěn jǐng jiāo　xiàng rú yǔ lián pō
- 刎颈交，相如与廉颇；

zǒng jiǎo hǎo　sūn cè yǔ zhōu yú
总角好，孙策与周瑜。

yǔ shàn rén jiāo　rú rù zhī lán zhī shì
- 与善人交，如入芝兰之室，

jiǔ ér bù wén qí xiāng
久而不闻其香；

yǔ èr én jiāo　rú rù bào yú zhī sì
与恶人交，如入鲍鱼之肆，

jiǔ ér bù wén qí chòu
久而不闻其臭。

cài yōng dào xǐ yǐ yíng bīn　zhōugōng wò fà ér dài shì
- 蔡邕倒屣以迎宾，周公握发而待士。

bó yá jué xián shī zǐ qī　gèng wú zhī yīn zhī bèi
- 伯牙绝弦失子期，更无知音之辈；

guǎn níng gē xí jù huà xīn　wèi fēi tóng zhì zhī rén
管宁割席拒华歆，谓非同志之人。

jià què qiáo yǐ dù hé niú nǚ xiāng huì
架鹊桥以渡河，牛女相会；

shè què píng ér zhōng mù táng gāo dé qī
射雀屏而中目，唐高得妻。

nù fà bīngguān lìn xiàng rú zhī yīng qì bó bó
怒发冰冠，蔺相如之英气勃勃；

zhì shǒu kě rè táng cuī xuàn zhī guì shì yán yán
炙手可热，唐崔铉之贵势炎炎。

jiǔ bù qū zī xī guō zǐ yí zūn jū zǎi xiàng
久不屈兹膝，郭子仪尊居宰相；

bú wèi mǐ zhé yāo táo yuānmíng bú bài lì xū
不为米折腰，陶渊明不拜吏胥。

lǎo dāng yì zhuàng nìng zhī bái shǒu zhī xīn
老当益壮，宁知白首之心；

qióng qiě yì jiān bú zhuì qīng yún zhī zhì
穷且益坚，不坠青云之志。

# 卷三

zhì yù yuán ór xíng yù fāng， dǎn yù dà ér xīn yù xiǎo
- 智欲圆而行欲方，胆欲大而心欲小。

míng xīn lòu gǔ， gǎn dé nán wàng
- 铭心镂骨，感德难忘；

jié cǎo xián huán， zhī ēn bì bào
结草衔环，知恩必报。

dí shèn yì cuī， yuē fā méng zhèn luò
- 敌甚易摧，曰发蒙振落；

zhì zài bì shèng， yuē pò fǔ chén zhōu
志在必胜，曰破釜沉舟。

mù xiè zhú tóu， jiē wéi yǒu yòng zhī wù
- 木屑竹头，皆为有用之物；

niú sōu mǎ bó， kě bèi yào shí zhī zī
牛溲马勃，可备药石之资。

máo suí piàn yán jiǔ dǐng， rén zhòng qí yán
- 毛遂片言九鼎，人重其言；

jì bù yí nuò qiān jīn　rén fú qí xìn
季布一诺千金，人服其信。

guǎnzhōng kuī bào　suǒ jiàn bù duō
管中窥豹，所见不多；

zuò jǐng guān tiān　zhī shí bù guǎng
坐井观天，知识不广。

hàn wǔ nèi duō yù ér wài shī rén yì
汉武内多欲而外施仁义，

lián pō xiān guó nàn ér hòu sī chóu
廉颇先国难而后私仇。

lín yuān xiàn yú　bù rú tuì ér jié wǎng
临渊羡鱼，不如退而结网；

yáng tāng zhǐ fèi　bù rú qù huǒ chōu xīn
扬汤止沸，不如去火抽薪。

ān bù ké yǐ dāng chē　wǎn shí ké yǐ dāng ròu
安步可以当车，晚食可以当肉。

xiào rén shàn wàng　yuē xǐ zhái wàng qī
笑人善忘，曰徙宅忘妻；

jī rén bù jǐn, yuē kāi mén yī dào
讥人不谨，曰开门揖盗。

kē zhōu qiú jiàn, gù ér bù tōng
刻舟求剑，固而不通；

jiāo zhù gǔ sè, jū ér bú huà
胶柱鼓瑟，拘而不化。

bá zhì lì zhì, hán xìn zhī jì shèn qí
拔帜立帜，韩信之计甚奇；

chǔ gōng chǔ dé, chǔ wáng suǒ jiàn wèi dà
楚弓楚得，楚王所见未大。

dǒng ān yú xìng huǎn, cháng pēi xián yǐ zì jí
董安于性缓，常佩弦以自急；

xī mén bào xìng jí, cháng pēi wéi yǐ zì kuān
西门豹性急，常佩韦以自宽。

mèngcháng lián jié, kè bǐ hé pǔ huán zhū
孟尝廉洁，克俾合浦还珠；

xiàng rú zhōngyǒng, néng shǐ qín tíng guī bì
相如忠勇，能使秦廷归璧。

yǐ xiǎo zhì dà　wèi zhī pāo zhuān yǐn yù

以小致大，谓之抛砖引玉；

bù zhī suǒ guì　wèi zhī mǎi dú huán zhū

不知所贵，谓之买椟还珠。

## 卷四

duō cái zhī shì　cái chǔ bā dǒu

多才之士，才储八斗；

bó xué zhī dé　xué fù wǔ chē

博学之德，学富五车。

jǐn xīn xiù kǒu　lǐ tài bái zhī wén zhāng

锦心绣口，李太白之文章；

tiě huà yín gōu　wáng xī zhī zhī zì fǎ

铁画银钩，王羲之之字法。

wǔ fèng lóu shǒu　chēng wén zì zhī jīng qí

五凤楼手，称文字之精奇；

qī bù qí cái　xiàn tiān cái zhī mǐn jié

七步奇才，羡天才之敏捷。

qín shǐ huáng wú dào fén shū kēng rú
秦始皇无道，焚书坑儒；

táng tài zōng hào wén kāi kē qǔ shì
唐太宗好文，开科取士。

kāi juàn yǒu yì sòng tài zōng zhī yào yǔ
开卷有益，宋太宗之要语；

bù xué wú shù hàn huò guāng zhī wéi rén
不学无术，汉霍光之为人。

zhōugōng dú zhì lǐ yuè xiāo hé zào lì lǜ tiáo
周公独制礼乐，萧何造立律条。

bǐ nǎi méng tián suǒ zào zhǐ nǎi cài lún suǒ wéi
笔乃蒙恬所造，纸乃蔡伦所为。

gōng shū zǐ xiāo mù yuān fēi tiān zhì sān rì ér bú xià
公输子削木鸢，飞天至三日而不下；

zhāngsēng yóu huà bì lóng diǎn jīng zé léi diàn ér fēi téng
张僧繇画壁龙，点睛则雷电而飞腾。

wú zhōngshēng yǒu yuē huà shé tiān zú
无中生有，曰画蛇添足；

jìn tuì liǎng nán yuē dī yáng chù fān
进退两难，曰羝羊触藩。

bēi zhōng shé yǐng zì qǐ cāi yí
杯中蛇影，自起猜疑；

sài wēng shī mǎ nán fēn huò fú
塞翁失马，难分祸福。

zhǐ lù wéi mǎ qín zhào gāo zhī qī zhǔ
指鹿为马，秦赵高之欺主；

chì shí chéngyáng huáng chū píng zhī dé xiān
叱石成羊，黄初平之得仙。

fú jiān wàngzhēn yí cǎo mù jiē shì jìn bīng
苻坚望阵，疑草木皆是晋兵；

suǒ jìng zhī wáng tàn tóng tuó huì zài jīng jí
索靖知亡，叹铜驼会在荆棘。

xiū mǔ huà dí yǐ jiào zǐ shuí bù chēng xián
修母画荻以教子，谁不称贤；

lián pō fù jīng yǐ qǐng zuì shànnéng huǐ guò
廉颇负荆以请罪，善能悔过。

mí zǐ xiá cháng shì chǒng jiāng yú táo yǐ dàn jūn
弥子瑕常恃宠，将余桃以啖君；

qín shāngyāng yù xíng lìng shǐ xǐ mù yǐ lì xìn
秦商鞅欲行令，使徙木以立信。

zhǔ dòu rán qí bǐ xiōng cán dì
煮豆燃萁，比兄残弟；

kǎn zhú zhē sǔn qì jiù lián xīn
砍竹遮笋，弃旧怜新。

**图书在版编目（CIP）数据**

《幼学琼林》故事：汉英对照／张梅著；畅国杰译.
—北京：五洲传播出版社，2009.12
（中国蒙学经典故事丛书）
ISBN 978-7-5085-1735-3

Ⅰ.①幼… Ⅱ.①张…②畅… Ⅲ.①汉语—对外汉语教学-语言读物 ②汉语—古代-启蒙读物
Ⅳ.①H195.5②H194.1

中国版本图书馆CIP数据核字（2009）第209392号

主　　编：荆孝敏　邓锦辉
副 主 编：王　峰
顾　　问：赵启正　沈锡麟　潘　岳
　　　　　周黎明（美）　李莎（加）　威廉·林赛（英）
监　　制：林武汉
著　　者：张　梅
翻　　译：畅国杰
责任编辑：王　峰
设计指导：缪　惟
设计制作：潘宏伟　林国霞
插　　图：刘向伟　刘　倩

**《幼学琼林》故事**

出版发行：五洲传播出版社
社　　址：北京市海淀区莲花池东路北小马厂6号华天大厦
邮政编码：100038
电　　话：010-58891281
传　　真：010-58891281
制版单位：北京锦绣圣艺文化发展有限公司
印　　刷：北京彩和坊印刷有限公司
开　　本：787x1092　1/16
印　　张：11.75
版　　次：2010年1月第1版　2010年1月第1次印刷
书　　号：ISBN 978-7-5085-1735-3
定　　价：79.00元